The Long Dark Trail

US Marshal Jubal Judd receives a request for help from Judge Geddings. The judge has seen a man called Rufus Wilton whom, fourteen years previously, Geddings sentenced to hang for murder. But before the sentence could be carried out, Wilton escaped, and he has now assumed the guise of a respected citizen.

But by the time Judd reaches Ashby he is too late. The judge has been shot and killed. And he left no clue as to who Wilton is posing as.

It is up to Judd to find and stop Wilton before he kills again. But he soon realizes he must face one of the most dangerous men around. Jubal will need more than luck if he is to get his man!

The Long Dark Trail

STEVEN GRAY

A Black Horse Western

ROBERT HALE · LONDON

© Steven Gray 2004
First published in Great Britain 2004

ISBN 0 7090 7542 1

Robert Hale Limited
Clerkenwell House
Clerkenwell Green
London EC1R 0HT

Typeset by
Derek Doyle & Associates, Liverpool.
Printed and bound in Great Britain by
Antony Rowe Limited, Wiltshire

CHAPTER ONE

Judge Theodore Geddings paused on the hotel porch. It was a lovely, sunny June morning, hot, but not as overpoweringly so up here in the high country as down in the desert. When he reached Ashby's main street, he stopped and decided his first impression of the town had been right. Ashby would make an ideal place to spend his approaching retirement, along with his daughter, Barbara, who had grown into a beautiful young woman when he wasn't looking. He felt sure she would like it here.

As he started on the short walk to the newly built courthouse, he was greeted by several passers-by. He acknowledged them, almost allowing himself to smile. He decided he would begin putting his affairs in order and then visit the real estate office, find out if they could offer him a suitable house or whether it would be best to have one built. Perhaps somewhere out by the river.

He came to a sudden halt, staring across the street at a man emerging from the dry-goods store. Confusion, disbelief flooded his mind. No, no, it couldn't be. Impossible. Not after all these years. And his thoughts fled back to the courtroom in Juniper Creek and the trial of Rufus Wilton.

'Foreman of the jury, how do you find the defendant, guilty or not guilty?'

'Damn guilty, Judge.'

The courtroom was crowded. The trial had attracted not only townsmen but others from miles around. Despite the expectant hush that had greeted Judge Geddings's words, not one man present was surprised at the verdict. Rufus Wilton might have pleaded his innocence to the charge of robbery and murder but no one doubted his guilt.

Not only was there the evidence against him: the money he shouldn't have had, his bloodstained clothes, the fact he owned the knife used to slit the throats of Adam and Maud Roberts. There was also his behaviour. The way he'd slumped, seemingly uninterested, in his seat during the two days of his trial. Yet no one had missed how his eyes lingered on each witness who spoke, as well as on judge and jury, as if he wanted to remember each and every one so that later he could take his revenge on them. Nor had they missed his smirk, as if he knew secrets no one else was aware of.

And it had been noted how the lawyer hired to defend Wilton had not tried very hard to prove him innocent. It was as if he was not only well aware of his client's guilt but wanted him locked up. In fact, now the verdict was in he looked relieved.

As a muttering of satisfaction broke out, Geddings

banged his gavel on the desk and called, 'Quiet, quiet!' He saw Marshal Hattersley hitch his gunbelt higher and nod at his deputy to be alert.

Trials were held in the back room of the saloon. It was the only place large enough and it had the added benefit of being near the one-celled jailhouse so there wasn't far to bring the accused. But it wasn't the most secure of places and obviously Hattersley didn't want any of the town's outraged citizens making a rush for Wilton and forcing him out to be lynched. Wilton was going to hang but both Geddings and Hattersley wanted it done all nice and legal.

The prisoner was a young man of nineteen with dark-brown hair, brown eyes and thin lips making his sneer all the more pronounced. He stood with his lawyer just a few feet away from the judge's desk. Geddings looked at him and Wilton stared straight back.

During the three years Geddings had ridden the legal circuit on the frontier, during the years before that serving as a judge in New York, he had presided over the trial of many a murderer. Mostly they had been thugs with little intelligence who knew no better, or those who had acted on an impulse they would regret until they were hanged: wild, quick-tempered or plain stupid. He'd never believed that those who murdered others were necessarily evil, never really believed in evil itself.

With Wilton he wasn't quite so sure. He thought it was foolish to feel there was anything different about the young man who stood before him, especially when he had been so easily captured. And yet he had a look in his eyes – a cunning cleverness, a ruthlessness, a . . . well, yes, evil was the word that came to mind.

Despite his age and experience, Geddings couldn't suppress a shiver of foreboding. A feeling made worse when he realized Wilton knew exactly what was on his mind. But what was he scared of, for what could happen? He'd never been afraid to impose the ultimate sentence. Within a week Wilton would hang and would no longer be able to hurt anyone.

Forcing his eyes away from the young man's mocking gaze, Geddings clutched his hands together on the desk top and raised his voice to address the court.

'It is my misfortune to have to say that in all my years as a judge I do not believe I have ever encountered a more heinous crime than the one before me now. You, Mr Wilton, entered a law abiding community, alone and penniless, were taken in and given shelter. You repaid this kindness by stealing from those who helped you. And when your crimes were discovered you killed without mercy. And have since shown no remorse.'

Hattersley's hand dropped to rest on the butt of his gun. Not only were there loud murmurs coming from the men gathered behind him but Wilton had started to fidget, was almost bouncing from one foot to the other. Was trying not to smile.

Frowning, Geddings lowered his voice trying to convey the seriousness of the situation to the prisoner.

'Even today, here in court, tried by your peers and

found guilty, you do not seem to realize what you have done. Or maybe you simply do not care. Well, young man, you will find that this court cares, it cares very much. I have no hesitation in passing the death sentence upon you. You will be taken from here back to the jailhouse and as soon as it can be arranged you will be conveyed from there to a place of execution and hanged by the neck until pronounced dead. Do you understand?'

'Yeah, sure, what's not to understand?' Wilton's voice was as mocking as his face. 'I ain't stupid.'

Geddings banged his gavel again to stop the angry mutterings this remark caused.

'And it is to be hoped you will find the time and opportunity to reflect upon what you have done and seek forgiveness.'

'Forgiveness, shit! I'll see you in hell first. I'll see you all in hell!'

And at that moment hell broke out in the courtroom. And the judge realized the danger didn't come from the onlookers, it came from the prisoner himself.

With a howl that caused the blood of those who heard it to turn cold, Wilton swung his handcuffed hands at his lawyer. The blow caught the man on the chin, causing him to stumble. At the same time Wilton leapt towards the judge.

Geddings shrank away while Hattersley dived in front of the desk, clawing at his gun.

If it had been Wilton's intention to attack the judge, he quickly changed his mind.

Instead he veered towards the deputy marshal. He

9

caught hold of the deputy's gunhand and hit him in the chest with his elbow, causing the man to grunt in pain. Wilton grabbed his gun and shot him in the stomach. As the deputy was falling, Wilton swung round, pointing the weapon at his lawyer.

'No! No, please!'

Wilton fired again, yelling, 'Useless sonofabitch, you shoulda done a better job!'

Amid yells of fright and confusion, he raced towards the door at the back of the court. He knocked aside one man who got in his way, shot another.

Hattersley raised his pistol.

'No, don't,' Geddings cried. 'You might hit some-one else.' Then it was too late. Wilton was through the door, slamming it shut behind him.

The shocked spectators picked themselves up from where they'd dived for cover. A couple of men went to see if they could help the lawyer while Hattersley moved towards his deputy.

Geddings stopped him.

'I'll see to things here. You get after the bastard.'

Hattersley ran through the saloon to the street. Close behind were several young men he could always rely on whenever he needed to form a posse.

Geddings found out later that outside it had been quiet, with most people indoors waiting out the hottest hours of the day. A few townspeople, attracted by the shooting, had gathered by the door of the general store on the opposite side of the plaza. Otherwise the street was empty.

Thinking that if Wilton had any sense he would

make a run for it, the posse hurried down to the livery stable, to find he had indeed been there before them. The gate of the corral out back was open and the few horses kept there had strayed into the dusty road. Pablo Morales, the stable-owner, lay in one of the stalls, a bullet hole in his shoulder.

As Wilton clearly intended, having to round up and saddle the horses delayed the posse. At last, Hattersley at their head, the men galloped out of town. They clattered across the rickety bridge over Juniper Creek, instantly finding themselves in the vast, endless Arizona desert which surrounded the town. Grey scrub flats stretched for miles, empty except for sagebrush and rocks, leading to the far mountains.

If Geddings hoped Hattersley would recapture Wilton he was doomed to disappointment.

'We chased the bastard for three long, hot days,' Hattersley told the judge when the posse returned to Juniper Creek, tired, dusty and dispirited. 'At first it was easy to follow his trail. But when we reached the foothills it was a different story.'

It was obvious Wilton hadn't cared if he was followed across the desert but had raced for the hills so he could employ any number of tricks to lose the posse there. And lose them he had.

The trail petered out amongst rocks and shale and despite all the posse's searching they couldn't find it again. They had no choice but to give up and return to Juniper Creek.

'I knew Wilton had escaped us when late in the afternoon we came across a pair of handcuffs. They

11

were hanging from the branch of a Joshua tree.'

Mocking them and their efforts.

Hattersley sighed. 'I'm sorry, Judge.'

Geddings nodded. Hattersley was a good man, he had done his best. But he was as worried as the marshal sounded. They both knew Wilton was the type to continue robbing and killing and he wondered whether there was something more either of them could or should have done to stop him.

Fourteen years! It was a long time. Could he be mistaken? Certainly the man he'd seen didn't look like Rufus Wilton. This man's hair and build were different and he was no longer the scrawny boy Geddings had sentenced to hang. But people changed. He himself had. His once brown hair and beard were now iron-grey. He walked with a stoop and sometimes he didn't hear what people said to him.

Some people said, hoped, Wilton had died out in the desert – of thirst, of an Indian attack or rattlesnake bite. Geddings had hoped so too but he'd never really believed it. Wilton was the type to survive. And as well as changing his appearance a man could change his name.

The trouble was, over the years he thought he'd recognized Wilton a number of times. And each time he'd been wrong. He could be wrong now.

All at once Geddings felt every bit of his sixty-five years. His plans were spoiled. Ashby was no longer ideal. Instead it harboured evil. And he didn't notice the sunshine any more for as far as he was concerned a shadow overhung the town.

He gave himself a mental shake. Such thoughts would do no good. He must do something. But what? Tell someone? Yet he had no proof. Confront the man? But no, he shook his head, he wouldn't do that because, he was ashamed to admit, he was too scared.

But if he had recognized Wilton then Wilton would surely know him. And he was scared of that as well. He hoped the man hadn't seen him. Certainly he'd given no indication of doing so.

As he reached the courthouse steps, Geddings realized waiting and worrying would do no good. If he was right then all the time he did nothing there was the chance Wilton might escape the clutches of the law again. If he was wrong then he had nothing to brood over.

So he, who was usually so decisive, made up his mind. If he daren't do anything himself he would have to seek the help of someone who would.

In the meantime he could seek out the local law, probe Marshal Doyle to discover what he knew about the man who, he was sure, used to be Rufus Wilton.

CHAPTER TWO

Rufus Wilton was annoyed with himself. He faced being found out and caught. It was his own fault. He shouldn't have stayed so long in Ashby. Should have made his plans and, having carried them out, moved on. He'd always kept on the move before, not run the risk of anyone discovering his real identity. But Ashby was the wealthiest town he'd ever been in. Most places were of no account with little to offer. Ashby had potential. And he enjoyed an easy life here.

And really how could he have figured the judge – Judge Geddings of all people, the bastard who considered him so bad he wanted him dead – would come here?

It was a nasty shock, seeing him, walking as large as life down Main Street. But, he grinned, it must have been an even bigger shock for Geddings. And the old man had recognized him, no doubt about that.

Still he had, as usual, been clever. Hadn't betrayed the fact he'd seen Geddings. With luck the judge wouldn't take any precautions. He'd always regretted not having shot him all those years ago back in

Juniper Creek. So, now, the sooner he put that right, the better.

It was crowded in the marshal's office. The room wasn't all that large and contained two desks, three chairs, a safe, gun cabinet and a table on which a pile of Wanted posters waited to be sorted out. A door at the back led through to two cells.

Marshal Simon Doyle sat at his desk, thinking that once it became cooler he'd have no excuse not to go out and start serving tax notices; a job destined to make him unpopular with the townsfolk.

Doyle was in his late twenties, an amiable-looking young man with bushy brown hair and blue eyes that missed very little. He'd been appointed town marshal because he was competent enough to get on with the job without any supervision and only one deputy. Not that Ashby presented much of a challenge. Mostly it was quiet with the little trouble there was confined to the small red-light district on the edge of town. He was able to handle everything easily enough.

He was glad to be interrupted by David Marston, a tall spindly man with a halo of fair hair, who was a clerk from the courthouse.

'What can I do for you?' Doyle said.

'Judge Geddings has asked if he could see you.'

'Sure.'

Judge Theodore Geddings had arrived in Ashby the day before. Doyle had been looking for an opportunity to introduce himself to the man who had ridden the frontier law circuit for so many years and done so much to help bring law and order to

Arizona; although if the number of Wanted posters that came in on every stagecoach from all corners of the West was anything to go by much more remained to be done.

As Doyle followed Marston outside, the sun striking hot, he said:

'Do you know what the judge wants?'

'No,' Marston said, then paused.

'What's the matter?'

'He seems worried about something.'

'Oh, what?'

'I don't know. I might be wrong. He hasn't said anything. It's only a feeling.'

The courthouse stood just beyond the marshal's office. It was a new building erected when the town council decided Ashby was important enough to have a proper court. It faced on to the street with a walled area at the rear. Inside, the courtroom took up half of the building and the other half contained several rooms where the varied work of the court took place. At the end of a short corridor was the room a visiting judge used when he was in residence.

Doyle swallowed, suddenly feeling rather nervous at the thought of coming face to face with such a renowned judge.

'Had you met Geddings before?' he asked Marston, wondering what the man was like.

The clerk shook his head.

'No, this is the first time he's visited Ashby and—'

A shot! Loud, echoing in the quiet of the building! Coming from Geddings's office. Followed by a cry, another shot and the thump of a body falling.

'Oh my God!' Marston cried in a horrified tone. 'Judge! Judge! What's happening?'

Even as he called out, Doyle was pushing by him, drawing his gun as he did so. The clerk was right behind him as he shoved the door open.

Marston exclaimed: 'Judge Geddings! Oh God!'

Beyond was a large room, with two windows, a desk and several chairs, even a bookcase. The judge's body was slumped on the floor, half-hidden by the desk. Around the body, blood was spreading across the floor.

The dark shadow of a man loomed over by one of the windows.

'Look out!' Doyle yelled.

The shadow fired once, twice, three times.

Doyle ducked down out of the way, thrusting the clerk behind him. Even as he fired back at the assailant, Marston gave a little moan and fell against him, spoiling his aim, before collapsing to the floor.

And the shadow had gone.

Doyle didn't pause. Whatever had happened to the judge and the clerk, whether they were dead or just wounded, he could do nothing for them. But he might be able to catch the person responsible. He gave chase.

The window looked out on to the small enclosed yard at the back of the courthouse. At the bottom trees grew along a high wall, hiding the jailhouse from view. He reached the window as the man reached the trees. He was aware that the man wore a long duster coat and had a scarf wrapped around his head and face making identification impossible.

Then there was no more time for thought. Doyle

scrambled through the opening and hit the ground, running and shooting. He swore as he missed his target. Had to weave out of the way as the man paused to fire back at him, a bullet coming so close he heard its whine in his ear.

Then the assailant was up and over the wall, dropping out of sight.

Doyle raced for the wall, jumped for the top and pulled himself up. He made sure he wasn't heading into an ambush before half-jumping, half-falling to the ground on the other side. He found himself in the dusty alleyway at the side of the jailhouse. A quick glance up and down. The man had disappeared.

The alley led in two directions. Which way? Probably not towards the street. The shots would attract attention. People would be coming to find out what they meant. The other way then.

Cautiously but swiftly, hugging the jailhouse wall, Doyle ran to the end of the alley. It opened out on to an empty lot with more buildings beyond. Empty too of the killer he was chasing.

He ran to the corner of the next building. No one. Nothing.

'Dammit!'

In the hope that he'd been wrong he ran back the other way. People were converging on the court-house from all directions. They surged forward, demanding to know what was going on.

When he'd managed to quieten them down, Doyle said:

'I'll tell you when I know what's happened myself. Now there ain't nothing for any of you here. Why don't you go on home?'

No one moved to obey him. There was no sign of his deputy, who being young and irresponsible, was never around when he was needed, but with some relief he saw Doctor Hicks near the front of the crowd.

'Hicks,' he called, 'come with me, will you? I need your help.'

'What is it?'

Doyle waited until Hicks got up to him and then said quietly so no one else would hear:

'Someone's shot Judge Geddings.'

'My God! Is he dead?'

'I don't know. That's why I need you. Yes, I think he is.'

The few staff who worked at the courthouse were gathered outside the judge's door, whispering to each other, faces lit up with horror and excitement. Doyle ushered them away. Inside, Marston had sat up and was leaning against the wall. He was white-faced with pain, clutching his arm. Blood had soaked into his jacket sleeve.

Another, older, clerk crouched over the judge's body, which still lay in the same position. The clerk looked up, shaking his head.

'He's dead. Shot in the back, with a second bullet in his side.'

'God,' Doyle muttered and swore several times, while Hicks went to make sure the clerk was right. 'Jesus, what a mess.' Doyle was so overcome with the seriousness of the situation that for the moment he didn't know quite what to do. He bent down by Marston. 'You hurt bad?'

'No.' But the man moaned. He was turning whiter by the minute, lips pinched together.

'You,' Doyle spoke to the clerk still bending down by the judge, 'can you fetch the undertaker?'

With a nod, the man hurried out.

'Marshal, what's wrong?' It was Doyle's deputy, Pat Fisher.

'Ah, Pat, there you are at last. Where've you been?'

'Sorry. I was down in the red-light district and didn't hear the commotion.'

'You were working, I hope?'

'Of course, Marshal.' But Fisher went very red so everyone knew he was lying.

'Never mind.'

By now Hicks had moved Marston to a chair against the wall.

'The bullet is in there but it's not a deep wound,' he said. 'You'll be all right.' He shut up his doctor's bag but made no move to leave.

'Marston, you up to answering some questions before you go with the doc?'

'Yes, sir.'

'You thought Geddings was worried?'

Marston gave a little nod. 'And he was most anxious to see you, although he didn't say why. Oh!'

'What?'

'Directly he arrived at the courthouse this morning he got me to take a letter down to the stagecoach office to catch the early stage.'

'What did it say? Who was it to?'

'It was to the United States Marshal for the area. A Jubal Judd.'

Doyle nodded. He'd heard of the man.

'But I don't know what it said. I never saw it. The judge wrote the message out himself and put it in a sealed envelope.'

'See here, Simon.' Hicks was over by the judge's desk. 'He was writing another letter.'

Doyle picked up the solitary piece of paper on the desktop. It was splotched with blood.

'It's addressed to someone called Hattersley. Does the name mean anything to either of you? It doesn't to me.'

Both Hicks and Marston shook their heads.

'He hadn't got very far. Just that he has an important piece of news for this Hattersley. Damn. I guess we'll have to wait to read the letter he sent to Judd and hope that tells us more.'

Hicks helped Marston to his feet. Marston grimaced and said, 'By the way, Marshal, Miss Geddings will have to be told.'

'Miss Geddings?'

'Yes, the judge's daughter. As far as I'm aware she's his only relative. At least out here. She'll have to decide what she wants done with her father's body.'

'Hell, yes. Do you know where she lives?'

'In Tucson. I don't know the address, but it'll surely be amongst the judge's papers at the hotel. Poor girl. This will be a dreadful shock.'

That this – the murder of a famous judge – should have happened in his town was a dreadful shock to Doyle as well!

CHAPTER THREE

'Ashby, folks!' the driver called out, pulling the Wells Fargo stagecoach to a halt.

It was mid-afternoon. Still hot, Jubal Judd thought sourly. He didn't like stagecoach travel, with its uncomfortable seats, other passengers who liked to gossip and, worst of all, the dust that blew in through the windows and covered everything. But taking the stagecoach was the quickest way for him to reach Ashby and the judge's letter had indicated a certain amount of urgency.

In order to get out of the sun Judd went to stand in the shade of the sidewalk while he waited for the driver to unload his carpetbag. Being vain about his appearance he banged what dust he could from his clothes and decided that, whatever the hurry, before going to see Judge Geddings he would book a room at a hotel and tidy up.

He wanted to change his clothes and comb the tangles out of his fair hair, which hung in curls down to his shoulders. Polish his boots until they shone. Make sure he looked tidy.

Just over six feet tall with broad shoulders, Judd had a fair moustache, which was always neatly trimmed, and light-brown eyes. As usual he wore a white shirt and black suit, the sombreness broken by a richly decorated vest, today's being deep red decorated with green swirls. His black Stetson had a small feather stuck in the band.

He was aware that some people called him a dandy and considered him full of his own importance. Until they dared say so to his face, which wasn't likely seeing how good he was with his fists and guns, he wasn't about to worry over the opinions of others.

Judd was one of the youngest men ever to be appointed a United States marshal, for he was still only in his early thirties. He was ambitious and determined to be successful, and not be accused of gaining the position through political leverage. Nor did he intend to sit behind a desk dealing with paperwork while the deputy marshals rode around gaining glory and advancement.

At the same time he didn't think much glory would be had from this assignment and if a deputy had been available Judd would have sent him to Ashby instead of coming himself.

Judge Geddings must be wrong. He was after all sixty-five. How could someone, a convicted killer, disappear for fourteen years, without committing any more crimes, and then resurface in a town like Ashby? It didn't seem likely. Much more likely this Rufus Wilton had died in the desert, been killed in a gunfight or perhaps faced a hangman under a different name.

But wrong, old, nearing retirement or not, Geddings was still a judge and a respected one at that; he had to be listened to. And the matter investigated.

'Marshal?'

Judd looked up to see a young deputy hovering by his side.

'Yeah?'

'I've been watching out for you. Our town marshal, Simon Doyle, would like a word please.'

'I'm on my way to see Judge Geddings.'

'It's about the judge he wants to see you. I'm afraid . . .' Pat Fisher paused and swallowed, unnerved by the marshal's hard glare.

'Well?'

'I'm afraid the judge is dead.'

'What!'

'He was shot and killed.'

Judd was stunned by the news, could hardly believe it.

'Jesus Christ, when?'

'Yesterday, sir. Marshal Doyle wants to talk to you about the letter the judge sent you.'

The hotel room and tidying up could wait. Judd needed to know what had happened.

'All right.'

'Here, let me take your bag. It's this way.'

The Wells Fargo stop was situated on the outskirts of the town and Judd, feeling dazed, wondering how and why the judge had been murdered, followed the deputy through a thriving business district to reach Main Street. Plenty of people were about: from cowboys, mostly hurrying to the saloons for a welcome cold beer, to sober-suited townsmen, while a number of women gossiped outside the stores.

There were plenty of stores too, selling all manner of goods. A bank. Two hotels. Café. Barber's shop. Neat sidewalks. Street lighting. The bell tower of a church glimpsed down a side-street. Everything was clean.

Ashby was a growing town.

Judd was impressed by it. He was also reasonably impressed with Simon Doyle, who looked capable enough; both clothes and gun being well-worn. Dismissing Pat Fisher, who looked thankful to escape the US marshal's stern presence, Doyle also quickly and clearly told him all about the judge's murder. When he had finished, Judd passed him the letter the judge had sent him.

It read:

Dear Marshal Judd,

In the past the United States Marshals' service has often helped me gain convictions in the cases I was responsible for judging. As you may know, I am now sixty-five but although approaching retirement I still sit before several courts. One of my fellow judges is sick at the moment and so I agreed to take his court here in Ashby, a place I have never before visited. I arrived yesterday. Now it seems I must again ask for help.

I am extremely worried. I believe I have seen here in town a man once known as Rufus

Wilton, who, fourteen years ago, I had the misfortune to try for theft and murder. He was found guilty and I sentenced him to hang. Before the sentence could be carried out he escaped custody and fled into the desert. To my knowledge no more was heard of him.

The point is, although I am certain in my mind it is the same man I have no proof beyond my own eyes. In fourteen years, Wilton has changed considerably and, more important, he now appears to be a respectable citizen. I would not want to make a fool of myself by accusing this person of being someone he is not or of committing a crime of which he is innocent.

I do not intend to ask the local marshal, whom I have every confidence is a good man able to handle town affairs competently, to investigate this matter. Partly because I think it would be unfair to expect him to do so and partly because I know town marshals are busy people. However, I shall find out what, if anything, he knows about this man. In the meantime, I would be grateful if you, or one of your deputies, could come to Ashby as soon as possible. You can then look into the matter for me and, I hope, provide evidence of the man's identity, one way or the other, and either arrest him or put my mind at rest that he is not who I think he is.

Yours respectfully,
Judge Theodore Geddings.

'But he didn't speak to you?' Judd asked.

'Unfortunately no.' Doyle shook his head. 'He was shot before I met him. I hoped his letter to you would tell me more. Instead it only seems to raise even more questions than it answers.' He glanced at it again. 'Rufus Wilton. I've never heard of him. Have you?'

'No. But there's no reason why we should. It was fourteen years ago, in a different part of the Territory and, as the judge states, no more has been heard of him.'

'This letter isn't very helpful, is it.' Doyle tapped the piece of paper. 'Hell, he doesn't say where the trial took place. Nor, more important, the name of the person he saw in Ashby.'

'No,' Judd agreed. 'Not helpful at all.'

'I've been trying to think of another reason for the judge being killed. That it might've been someone he jailed seeking revenge. Or friends or family of someone he sentenced to hang. But I suppose there ain't any doubt the judge did see this Wilton and Wilton shot him?'

Judd shrugged. 'It could have been someone with a grudge against him but I think that's too much of a coincidence. I believed Geddings was wrong, especially after so long, but it seems he was very right. Wilton must have recognized him too and shot him before he could say anything to anyone.'

'Yeah, that's the likeliest explanation,' Doyle agreed with a little nod. 'I wonder who the judge meant? I guess it was someone passing through whom Geddings happened to spot. We get a lot of drummers and such coming to town. Or it could've been a cowboy looking for work.'

'No, Doyle,' Judd objected, 'think about it. His letter mentions a respectable citizen. Someone you might know. That sounds as if he lives in Ashby. Or he's maybe a rancher.'

'I guess you're right,' Doyle admitted reluctantly. He frowned. 'It's a helluva shame he didn't name his suspect. I wonder why not.'

'Maybe he thought it would be best not to put it in writing. Or maybe he wrote the letter so quickly he simply forgot. It could even be that he was in such a hurry to seek help he didn't have time to learn the name Wilton was using. Perhaps he intended asking you.'

'Yeah, maybe. Although in that case how did he know the man was a respectable citizen?'

'Good point,' Judd agreed. 'Well, we've got to find out who he is. Somehow.'

'It could be almost anyone.' Doyle spoke gloomily, although he was pleased that Judd sounded as if he intended to include him in the investigation.

'Unfortunately, yeah. You said you didn't recognize the killer when you chased him?'

Doyle shook his head. 'He was wrapped up in a duster coat and scarf. I couldn't tell what he looked like.'

'If he was wearing a disguise of sorts it must mean you know him.'

Doyle couldn't think that that was particularly helpful but didn't like to contradict a US marshal.

'Did you notice if the killer had any blood on his clothes?'

Again Doyle shook his head.

'It happened so quickly. But Doctor Hicks said it was likely he would have. I've asked Pat, that's Pat Fisher, my deputy, to look for bloodstained clothing. But he hasn't found any yet.' He didn't sound hopeful.

'Well he might be lucky or, of course, the killer could have burned or buried anything incriminating. What about the direction you chased him, any clue there?'

'No. The bastard kept out of sight and was clever enough not to leave any traces behind.' Doyle paused. 'But I think maybe Old Roger—'

'Old Roger?'

'Yeah, Roger Turner. He works at the livery and I think he might have seen something. One alley comes out by the back of the stables where it's usually quiet with no one much around. He denied having seen anything but from the way he was acting I think he might be lying. He's a cantankerous old bastard and it would amuse him to lie to the law.'

'OK, we'll need to speak to him again. What else?'

Doyle hoped that Judd wouldn't find fault with what he had done or point out something simple that Doyle had stupidly left undone.

'I searched the judge's room at the Planter's Hotel. He was an experienced frontier traveller and travelled light but I did find some of his papers.'

Journals, notebooks and odd pieces of paper. All jammed together. All scribbled on. Even a quick glance had revealed they were not in any sort of order: of date, place or importance.

'I gave them to Marston, that's the clerk who was shot, to sort out.' Doyle didn't like paperwork. 'Maybe, with any luck, he'll come across the place where the trial of this Wilton was held, or even the name Hattersley.'

'Either would be helpful.. It seems to me we need to find out more about this Wilton and what he did before we can hope to discover who he is now.'

'What do you want to do first?'

'I'd better have a word with this Marston.'

'OK. He's at the courthouse. I'll take you and introduce you.'

CHAPTER FOUR

Judd might have been surprised when on their way to the courthouse they were joined by Doctor Hicks but Doyle wasn't. Hicks had a reputation for knowing when anything was happening in the town and, despite being busy with his doctoring, being determined to find out more.

He was a tall, thin man. Later Doyle said he was in his early thirties, although he looked and acted older. He had brown hair and grey eyes behind round spectacles. Judd thought Ashby was lucky to have a resident doctor, most frontier towns didn't have one. Or maybe Hicks had some reason of his own for coming here where he couldn't have earned as much money as if he'd gone somewhere like Santa Fe or Denver.

To Judd's considerable annoyance he accompanied the two lawmen into the courthouse and stood by while Judd was introduced to David Marston. His excuse appeared to be that he wanted to check the clerk's wound.

'You look better today,' he pronounced.

'I feel better, thanks, Doc, but it's a damn nuisance having my arm in a sling.'

'It won't be for much longer.'

'How are you getting on with the judge's papers?' Doyle asked.

Marston turned to him.

'Not very well, I'm afraid. I'm still trying to sort them out and I haven't come across anything useful yet.'

'I'd like to see where the judge was shot,' Judd said.

'Yes, sir, it's this way.'

Blood still stained the floor where Geddings had lain. Judd went over to the window and stared out.

'Did anyone else who works in the courthouse see anything?' No one else could have done for the courthouse was the only building to overlook the small garden.

'No,' Doyle said. 'I've questioned everybody. They were all busy and didn't realize anything was wrong until they heard the shots.'

Judd turned to the clerk.

'Geddings never said anything to you or the other clerks here about this Rufus Wilton?'

The man shook his head.

'Perhaps he felt he didn't know us well enough to confide in us.'

'I met him soon after his arrival,' Hicks said importantly.

Judd didn't miss the small smile exchanged by Doyle and Marston. Perhaps Doctor Hicks always made a point of getting to know any newcomer to

Ashby, especially one as important as the judge.

'He certainly never said a word to me.'

'Marston, who knew you were going to fetch Marshal Doyle?'

'No one. Or at least I don't think so. I mean Judge Geddings called me in, asked me to fetch the marshal as a matter of urgency and so I went straight away to find Mr Doyle.'

'You didn't tell anyone else where you were going or why?'

'No.' Marston spoke indignantly.

'Was the killer actually in the room?' Judd looked out of the window again.

'No.' It was Doyle who replied. 'At least not when me and Marston got in here. He was outside by then.' The clerk nodded his agreement. 'Of course he might have been in the room when he shot the judge. But most likely he simply shot him through the window.'

'I'm sure the judge had it open to let in some air,' Marston added.

'There doesn't seem to be any more to be seen here,' Judd decided. Doyle had said he had searched the judge's hotel room so there was little point in going there either. The marshal had been thorough in all he'd done.

'I'll keep going through the papers,' Marston promised.

'OK,' Doyle said. 'Let either me or Mr Judd know straight off if you find anything.' He led the way outside.

'Well I suppose I must be off,' Hicks said reluctantly as if he couldn't think of any good reason to linger.

Just at that moment a man wearing black and a clerical collar came into view, hurrying down the street towards them.

'The Reverend Oliver Stroud of Saint Anne's church,' Doyle told Judd.

A church and a permanent preacher as well as a doctor! Most impressive!

'Windbag,' Hicks put in.

'But he means well, Doctor. You can't deny he's done a great deal of work at the church since his arrival and he's always out and about visiting his parishioners.'

'Poking his nose in.'

As Stroud came closer, Judd thought he looked as if he was in his late thirties. He had dark-brown hair cut very short, brown eyes and a short brown beard. And a very serious face as if he seldom found much to smile about.

'Marshal Doyle. Doctor. Marshal, how are you getting on with finding the judge's murderer? You know he must be found and quickly otherwise Ashby's reputation will suffer.'

'He will be,' Doyle said and, as Stroud looked expectantly at Judd, introduced the two men.

'I don't suppose the judge spoke to you?' Judd said.

'Why no, no I'm afraid . . . I'm sorry to say I never had the chance to meet him. I meant to call on him but I never . . . in the very short time he was here, there wasn't time.'

'Too busy, I suppose,' Hicks muttered.

Stroud passed one hand in front of his face and stroked his beard.

'You know, Mr Judd, in many ways Ashby is a godless town. It has a thriving red-light district full of saloons and, I'm afraid to say, brothels too, that are all only too well frequented. There is a great deal of drunkenness especially on a Saturday night, even a gunfight now and then, usually over some prostitute.'

Doyle scowled as if he felt this was some sort of criticism of him.

'But in other ways it is a god-fearing place. The people were anxious for a church to be built so they could worship properly and I'm pleased to be here to help them.'

A grunt from Hicks.

'And on Sundays most people, both from the town and from the ranches and farms nearby, attend at least one of my services. If only to repent their sins so they can start sinning all over again on Monday! Perfect none of them is by any means but I find it hard to believe that a member of my congregation could be so sinful as to commit a cold-blooded murder.'

'Nevertheless the judge was murdered.' Hicks spoke sharply.

Stroud turned to the doctor, acknowledging what he said.

'Oh my, yes, of course. Dreadful! It's all been so difficult to take in.' He glanced across at Doyle before saying to Judd, 'Perhaps, Marshal, it's a good job you're here.'

Judd had the feeling that what he meant was that Doyle was only a town marshal and while he might be capable of handling the sort of work which that office entailed he probably wasn't up to handling a murder. If Doyle's frown was anything to go by he thought the man meant that as well.

'By the way, Doyle,' Stroud went on, 'have you heard any more from Miss Geddings?'

Doyle nodded.

'Yeah. She's on her way. I reckon if the stagecoach is on time she should be here some time tomorrow afternoon.'

'Good. I hope I shall be able to comfort her in her time of sorrow.'

After a few more minutes both reverend and doctor took the hint that their presence wasn't required any more and that they had no choice but to leave. Neither looked very happy at their dismissal and both parted company as soon as they were able.

As they started down the road, Judd asked what Marston and Hicks were like.

'Marston has worked at the courthouse for quite a while and is well trusted and well liked.'

'He couldn't have been involved, could he?' Judd was thinking of how Marston had fallen against Doyle just when he was going to shoot the killer.

'Oh no, I'm certain not. As for Hicks,' Doyle grinned, 'as you probably gathered, he likes to know what's going on. In fact, while he admits to being curious, most folk would call him downright nosy. He not only wants to know everything that's going on around Ashby, as its doctor he feels it's his right to know!'

Judd frowned. He didn't like the thought of a townsman interfering in the business of the law and intended to do all he could to keep Hicks away from it.

Doyle must have seen his look because he quickly added:

'I know Hicks can be a bit of a nuisance but he's harmless and everyone puts up with him because he's a good doctor. A doctor of any kind, let alone a good one, is pretty hard to find. And harder to keep.'

Which was clearly a warning for Judd not to do or say anything to annoy Hicks and perhaps make him think of leaving Ashby. As far as Judd was concerned, it depended on the circumstances. If they dictated he should annoy Hicks, he'd annoy him.

'Do you know where he's from? Why he's here?'

'Not really,' Doyle admitted with a little shrug. 'I know he's not very old but he seems to have been around for ever.'

'And the Reverend Stroud? Hicks doesn't seem to like him very much.'

'Before Stroud arrived, six or seven months ago now, Hicks was the one everyone went to for advice or help. Of a general nature as well as medically I mean. Now they sometimes go to Stroud. Hicks's nose has been put out of joint. Having said that, Stroud is a bit of a sanctimonious know-it-all.'

'How did he get to come here?'

'Generous donations meant a church had been built for some while but it was empty. The only time services were held was when a travelling preacher came to town. In the end it was decided that was stupid. There was no point having a church and not using it. So advertisements were placed in newspapers both in the East and in California for a minister to come live here. Stroud was chosen from several replies. He comes from California, somewhere near to San Francisco. Why?'

'No reason. Except it's a surprise for you to have a preacher living here in town. And a doctor.'

'I know,' Doyle agreed. 'Put it down to the town council. They work tirelessly to place Ashby on the map. There's even talk of a school and perhaps a theatre.'

CHAPTER FIVE

'Here, Barbara dear, drink this, it'll make you feel better.' Nora Wood put a cup of coffee that she had liberally laced with whiskey down on the table. She reached out to touch the girl's hand.

Barbara Geddings turned from where she had been staring out of the window of the stagecoach way station and smiled wanly.

'Thank you.' With a sigh she pushed aside her plate of almost untouched bacon and beans. 'Oh, Nora.'

'I know, dear. But we should be in Ashby tomorrow and we can find out exactly what happened once we get there.'

'I hope so.'

As soon as they received Marshal Doyle's telegram Barbara had decided she must visit Ashby. Left to herself she would have ridden all the way. It would have been quicker and easier but knowing she couldn't ask Nora to undertake such a journey she'd agreed to travel by stagecoach. A long, wearing trek, riding in the bumpy stage day and night with only short stops when the horses were changed.

Barbara hadn't wished to talk to anyone, especially strangers, about why she was so upset and luckily only two other passengers had caught the stage. One had left the coach at the previous stop and the other was a young cowboy, too shy to speak to either woman. She had not even wanted to remain at home to receive her friends and neighbours wishing to convey their sympathies but had wanted to set out as soon as possible. And tomorrow, at last, they would be in Ashby.

Barbara was twenty-one. She was nice-looking with light-brown hair secured in a tidy bun, brown eyes and a rosebud mouth. She had a good figure shown off by her clothes which were always designed in the latest style.

'Thank goodness you're here with me, Nora,' she said.

'And where else would I be, my girl?' Nora fetched her own cup of coffee and sat down.

Barbara acknowledged what she said with a little smile. Nora was now in her forties, with grey hair and light-blue eyes. She had become the family's house-keeper on the arrival of Barbara and her mother on the frontier. But she was much more than that, she was also Barbara's friend. And while Barbara knew it was selfish of her she was glad Nora had never remarried after the death of her husband in an Apache raid, but had remained in Tucson with her.

Barbara took a sip of coffee, feeling its warmth settle into the pit of her stomach. Her mind was in a whirl. What had happened? How could her father,

Judge Theodore Geddings, be dead? Shot to death! Murdered! It was impossible. Tears came into her eyes and she sighed unhappily.

Aware of Nora looking very worried, she said:

'I'm all right. I was just thinking. It seems so wrong that father lived all those years amongst lawbreakers, judging and sentencing them, in some of the worst towns on the frontier and was never once harmed. Now he's getting ready to retire and settle down at last and he's killed. It's not fair.'

Nora nodded in agreement.

'He certainly worked hard enough to deserve a long and peaceful retirement.'

The door opened and the stagecoach guard came in.

'Ready to go, folks.'

Barbara hurried to finish her coffee and stood up, walking with Nora out to where the stage waited for them.

As the evening turned to dusk and then to night, both Nora and the young cowboy closed their eyes and fell into an uncomfortable doze. But as the stage bounced and swayed along the road, Barbara stayed awake, staring out of the window. Earlier that day they had left the empty rangeland behind and entered greener and cooler cattle country, but now there was little to see in the darkness except for trees and rocks crowding close on either side.

While she was shocked and upset about her father, Barbara also acknowledged to herself that she wasn't devastated. She had grown up a little afraid of the man with his hard eyes and stern bearing. Had felt at times he was judging her and probably finding her wanting. In truth, part of her had remained afraid when he proposed that once he retired she should live with him.

But the other part of her had been looking forward to talking to him; something she had found difficult as a child. She wanted to get to know him at last.

For all the while she was growing up he'd been too busy sitting as a judge, first in New York City and later riding round the frontier, to spend much time with his family.

Although she'd been little more than a baby she could remember everyone saying how foolish he was when he decided to leave New York, where he enjoyed considerable wealth and prestige, and travel West. But he believed he was needed there, felt he could do a good job in ridding the frontier of its undesirables. He never doubted his decision. With a little smile she also remembered the considerable furore when he determined that his wife and only child should join him. In Arizona of all places! Tucson! It was unheard of.

And most of all her mother was against the idea. Was scared of the stories of Apache Indians and was sure they would either be scalped or killed by the outlaws who skulked behind every bush. But Barbara had been young enough to think of it as an exciting adventure.

Her mother had never taken to Tucson, to the heat and dust, the sometimes uncouth manners she encountered, the lack of society. But, like her father,

Barbara had never missed New York. She loved the West, knew it enabled her to have a much freer upbringing than she could have enjoyed in the city where relatives and neighbours would have looked askance at some of her wilder behaviour, would have been ready to reprimand her. Out here much was forgiven her because she was a good-looking young woman.

She sighed again, realizing, not for the first time, how much more like her father than her mother she was. Determined she thought; stubborn was the opinion of others.

Geddings had married late in life and Barbara's appearance was a considerable surprise to him. Most people thought he should never have married at all, was certainly not suited to become a father.

And perhaps they were right. For once she and her mother had reached Arizona he hardly ever visited them, even though he knew how difficult his wife found her new life. He hired Nora to look after them both and thought that was the end of his responsibility. When he did come home he was anxious to return to his work.

He was always a stranger to Barbara and had become more so since her mother's death two years ago.

Now it was too late. She would never know him. And he would never know her.

CHAPTER SIX

'Buy you a drink, Mr Judd?' Doyle asked.

Judd paused. He wanted to start the investigation but at the same time it was getting late. People were shutting up the stores and going home. He still had to get a room at the hotel. And suddenly he realized he was both hungry and thirsty. Maybe it would be best to leave doing anything more until tomorrow. And there were a few questions he could ask the marshal over a beer or two.

'OK, thanks.'

The red-light district was situated out beyond the business area. It wasn't very large and its one street ran down towards the river. There were four saloons of varying sizes and styles, two brothels and a billiards parlour. Already quite a number of young men were wandering up and down the sidewalks and several horses stood tied to the hitching rails.

'Some of the townsfolk want the area closed down,' Doyle said. 'They think its immoral.'

'Led by Reverend Stroud?'

'Exactly. But heck, most of the time people come here just to have a drink and relax and don't cause any problems. And the cowboys and younger towns-men need a place to let off steam. This way it's all contained in one area. Anyway, Stroud will be unlucky. It brings the town too much money for members of the council to want it closed.'

Judd thought the man was right on both counts.

Doyle led the way into The Retreat. It was the smallest saloon and respectable, with no gambling of any kind and only two extremely discreet prostitutes. A piano in one corner was being played enthusiasti-cally if not very well by a derby-hatted gentleman in his sixties. The few people drinking there were townsmen rather than cowboys.

While Judd sat down at a table by the window, the marshal bought them both beers, which was good and cold, and fetched over a plate of free hard-boiled eggs.

After a couple of sips, Judd put down his glass and leaned forward.

'Wilton escaped fourteen years ago,' he said, quietly so no one else would hear. 'That means he must have arrived in Ashby some time since then. In between he would have had to change his name and appearance. So, say, at a guess he can have been here no longer than ten years.'

Doyle frowned. 'That ain't much help.'

'Why not?'

'Ashby barely existed ten years ago. Let alone four-teen. Even up till three or four years ago it was little more'n a trading-store and a couple of saloons catering to the ranchers who were then in the area. And there weren't many of them either. While one or two came here straight after the Civil War most are more recent arrivals. A few farmers have followed in their wake. As far as I know no one was in this particular part of the country before the War.'

'It's grown rapidly, then?'

'Yeah. And on the whole it's a good town with mostly good folks.'

'Were you here from the beginning?'

'No, I'm a fairly recent arrival. I was a deputy marshal over in New Mexico. Small town you probably haven't never heard of. But I liked the idea of being a marshal. So I came here. Up till now there ain't been any trouble I can't handle. But this.' Doyle shook his head. 'I ain't so sure about this.' He looked at Judd. 'I'm afraid I'm out of my depth. I'm glad you're here.'

'I hope we can work together,' Judd said. He would be the one in charge but it never hurt to have the help and goodwill of the local law.

Doyle nodded.

'What made Ashby take off?'

'Rumours began to flow about a railroad line coming through,' Doyle said with a smile.

'There's no sign of one.'

'No. I don't think there was ever meant to be one. But luckily the town continued to grow because people realized it was situated in an ideal spot with plenty of water and good grazing land. And these days rumours abound about the railroad putting in a spur line.' Doyle grinned. 'I have a feeling that's more to do with the town council than what might really happen.'

'Your town council is real busy then?'

'Oh yeah!'

From the way he said that Doyle must sometimes wish them to be less busy.

'Who's on it?'

'Doctor Hicks for one. Well, you might know he would be! Its leader is Bruce Anderson who owns the dry goods store. He's a good organizer. It was his idea and his work that got us the church. There's a couple of other members. Browning, the telegraph operator and John Proctor. Strictly speaking he shouldn't be on the town council because he's a rancher.'

'So why is he?'

'Apart from the fact that he's a goddamn nuisance and while he's not the biggest rancher in the area he would like to be?'

'Yeah, apart from that.'

Doyle finished his beer. 'I guess there are many ranchers around here who are as successful as Proctor but they don't shout their mouths off like he does. Of course, he is wealthy, although that's partly because he's so damn mean, and he believes his wealth gives him certain rights, which I suppose it does.' He sighed. 'I just bet a meeting will be called as soon as possible with demands that the killer is caught quickly.'

Judd decided that if this Proctor, or any other members of the town council, tried to demand anything of him they would get short shrift. He went to buy them more beer and when he got back to the table, said:

'I wonder why Wilton has come here. If there's any special reason.'

'It's a fairly prosperous place.'

'That's what I mean. Has anything been happening around town that's gotten you worried?'

'What sort of thing?' Doyle frowned, obviously not understanding what Judd was getting at.

'I just think that Wilton sounds like someone who won't be able to give up thieving and killing wherever he goes and whatever he calls himself. Have you had any trouble like that lately?'

'Hmmm,' Doyle said thoughtfully. 'Well, apart from the judge, there ain't been any recent murders in Ashby or nearby. There was a fatal stabbing in one of the brothels a few weeks ago but that was due to a fight over a whore and easily dealt with. Otherwise it's been pretty quiet. We've got our share of the rowdy and wild but most of the cowboys've been away on spring round-up and driving the herds to the railhead. They've only just started drifting back.'

'What about robberies?'

'Well, yeah, of course there's always robberies of one kind or another. But I guess you don't mean petty thefts?'

Judd shook his head; he didn't.

'There was one robbery, let me see, a month or so ago. A little way out of town. Eddie and Sally Carmichael. Youngish couple who own a very small ranch. Not a lot was stolen but whoever did it caused a lot of damage to their place. Luckily the couple

48

were here in town at the time so they weren't hurt. I thought it was drifters, kids probably, and I never did find the culprits. You think that might've been Wilton?'

'I don't know,' Judd said with a shrug. 'You might be right about it being drifters. Although we know Wilton's a thief we don't know what kind. He could be a bank or train-robber. We need to know more about him.' Judd paused. 'Now you've had more time to think about everything is there anyone you know of who could once have been Wilton?'

'No. I ain't saying no one here in Ashby couldn't be capable of killing. But a cold-blooded killer?' Doyle shook his head. 'No, at least not as far as I know. What're you going to do now, Mr Judd?'

Judd leant back in his chair and thought for a moment or two.

'First thing tomorrow morning I'll speak to this Roger Turner, was it? – at the livery. See if you're right about him knowing something he refused to tell you.'

Doyle thought that if the marshal's face was anything to go by Old Roger wouldn't dare refuse to tell Judd!

'And perhaps when the judge's daughter gets here she might be able to tell us something useful.' Judd drank down his beer.

'Anything you want me to do?'

'Apart from avoiding the members of the town council?'

'Yeah,' Doyle agreed with a grin.

'You can keep an eye on David Marston, make sure

he doesn't miss anything in the judge's papers. Think if anyone in town has been acting suspiciously. Look through your Wanted posters. Keep Hicks and Stroud off my back.'

'OK.'

'And, Simon, be careful. I've got a real bad feeling about all this. The sooner it's cleared up the better.'

Doyle nodded. 'I agree.'

Judd stood up. 'I'll see you tomorrow.'

Doyle watched him leave. He didn't stay much longer himself.

Although a few people were still about, the streets were mostly quiet as Judd walked back to Main Street. He collected his bag from the marshal's office where Pat Fisher had left it and made his way down to the small hotel situated on the corner by the drugstore. He pushed open the door and entered the lobby. Inside it smelt of polish. Several chairs were dotted around the room. A clerk looked up from a desk in the corner and eyed him rather nervously. Judd couldn't decide whether the man was nervous of him or his two guns in their fancy leather holsters and the Winchester rifle poking out of his carpetbag.

'I'd like a room,' he said.

'How long for?'

'Not sure. A few days. Maybe longer.'

'Very well, Marshal. Sign the book.' The clerk looked a bit disappointed when Judd did so, perhaps hoping that he wouldn't be able to read or write. 'A bath is ten cents extra. I run a respectable hotel, Mr Judd. No boots in the bed, no spitting, or women in your room. And no firing your guns indoors.'

50

'I'll try to remember. Any chance of something to eat?'

The clerk sighed huffily; some guests were nothing but trouble! But he did promise to make sandwiches and coffee.

'Room six at the top of the stairs.' He handed Judd a key.

Judd went up the stairs which had a strip of red carpet running down the middle. In the hallway at the top was a round table with some flowers in a blue vase on it and an open window at the far end, letting in some much needed cool air.

His room looked out on to the side-street and was clean and neat, with a large bed, a chair and a wash-stand with a towel and bar of soap. A rag-rug lay in the middle of the floor and several hooks and shelves were provided for clothes.

Judd unpacked the few possessions he'd brought with him and then sat by the window, looking out on the quiet night, and eating the food the clerk reluctantly provided. He was anxious because as he'd said to Simon Doyle he didn't like the feel of this. And he couldn't wait for the morning so he could begin asking questions. Perhaps with luck Old Roger might tell him what he needed to know.

CHAPTER SEVEN

On the day Judge Geddings was shot, from the door of the livery Roger Turner had watched the approach of Marshal Doyle. He'd smiled but it was a sly smile that didn't reach his eyes. And he'd lied to Doyle when he said no, he hadn't seen anything. It was obvious the marshal had no idea of who was responsible for the murder. Hard luck for Doyle but maybe a bit of luck for himself.

Turner was in his sixties, with grey hair and a long grey beard. And a bent back. He was almost crippled from an old riding accident that had forced him to give up breaking horses and take up various odd and ill-paid jobs.

According to Turner he'd never had anything. Had always lived a hand-to-mouth existence, been put upon by others. Had to do those jobs others didn't like. The rancher he'd worked for had thrown him out when he was no more use. He was aware everybody called him Old Roger and he hated them for it.

Even now he didn't own the livery but ran it for

the town council and while he was paid a reasonable wage, he didn't consider it generous enough considering how wealthy Ashby was and how many hours he had to work: up early, late to bed, at everyone's beck and call. He felt he had to rely on tips, which were few and far between, to make a half-way decent living.

None of it was his fault, it was the fault of everyone else for never treating him right.

Since the shooting all that could soon change.

Standing in the shadows by the stables he'd watched the killer run out of the nearby alley, cross the dusty strip of land by the empty corral, and disappear round the back of the feed-and-grain store.

Should he have told the marshal whom he'd seen? But why should he? The marshal had no more time for him than anyone else. Anyway it was so incredible he doubted he'd be believed. He was sorry about the judge but at the same time he didn't know the man and nothing could bring him back.

So why shouldn't he profit from what he'd witnessed? Why should he help those who looked down on him as a no-account; called him a moaner.

With money in his pocket he could go somewhere he'd be appreciated. And the killer had better pay up or else Turner *would* go to the law, see him hanged, no mistake about that.

But for all his determination it had taken him some while to pluck up courage to face the killer. But now that fancy US marshal had arrived in town and, with more brains than poor old Doyle, might work out who was responsible. Fear of losing out, yet again, had made up his mind.

He'd do it that very night.

And, wouldn't you know it, that night he was busier than usual, having to work later than ever. But at long last he'd seen off the last of his customers and could shut up the stable for the night. He debated on whether to go home first but could see no reason to do so. Still, needing courage, he did pause long enough to finish off the whiskey he'd been sipping.

Except for those gathered in the red-light district no one was around. Everywhere else was closed and quiet. There was nobody to see him or wonder what he was doing or where he was going.

Although no one would ever have realized it from his behaviour, it had taken Rufus Wilton a long while to calm down after shooting the judge. He kept going over each detail again and again in his mind. How the man had turned in his chair, seen him standing outside the window, gun raised. Known what was about to happen and been powerless to stop it. He would savour for ever the look on the old man's face, the fear and anger in his eyes. Remember all that blood. It was about the best thing he'd ever done, although some of his other exploits did come close.

Of course, his troubles might not be over. A US marshal, no less, had arrived in town. Not that Jubal Judd with his fancy clothes and long hair looked as if he posed a threat. Even so it might be best to deal with him promptly because as Wilton was only too

54

well aware appearances could be deceptive. And there was the judge's daughter to consider. She might know all about Rufus Wilton. No matter. If so she could be dealt with as well.

But he supposed that while risks were all very well – dammit, at times they were thrilling and fun! – there also came a time when they were *too* damn risky and it was best to cut and run.

Reluctantly, Rufus Wilton decided that that time was fast approaching. Although people were so easy to fool and he didn't really believe he was anywhere near to being found out, he'd best leave Ashby, profitable though the town was, before there was any danger of his true identity being discovered. Go somewhere else where he could assume another identity.

But not quite yet. Before he left he had to find the opportunity to kill several of those who'd upset him, and especially find time to rob the Proctor family.

John Proctor lived with his wife, Alice, and their two young sons on a large spread some six miles out of town. They had arrived in the area several years ago and Wilton had visited the ranch once to check on whether the tales of the man's success and wealth were true. He'd liked what he'd seen. There were a great number of fat cattle grazing on the range and sleek horseflesh in the corral.

That wasn't all. According to gossip Proctor was mean. He didn't like spending money, didn't like paying cowboys and, except for round-up time, did most of the work himself. He was also a snob and the few men he did employ were kept well away from the ranch house. Certainly Wilton's visit had seemed to bear the rumours out. There was no sign of any cowboys around the place.

So what did he do with the money he made? Further rumour had it he hid it under his mattress.

Wilton smiled to himself. That rumour might or might not be true. It was worth investigating. And if Proctor was so mean he kept his money only to count it he couldn't really need it, whereas if Wilton was to leave Ashby behind he'd need money to help speed him on his way.

Not only that but Proctor was an opinionated sonofabitch and his wife a pious do-gooder. It would be pleasing to punish them both.

Wilton had a lot to do in the next few days and he decided all of it would be immensely enjoyable.

He wasn't happy when a knock at the door disturbed his memories and his plans. He was even less happy to see an idiot like Roger Turner on his doorstep. Old Roger was always whining on about how unfair his life was. Wilton often thought it would be kind to put the old fool out of his misery; kind to everyone else that was. What did he want?

That quickly became obvious with the man's first words:

'I seen you.'

'You'd better come in then.' Wilton opened the door wider and ushered Turner inside. 'Now, Mr Turner, you saw me where and doing what?'

He spoke lazily, not betraying any emotion, although his heart skipped several beats because, of course, he knew straight away what Turner meant.

He hadn't spotted the old fool when he ran out of the alley near to the livery stable but the man must have been there. Unfortunately for Turner they weren't beats of apprehension but of excitement and anticipation.

Turner stepped into the hallway.

'I seen you,' he repeated. 'Running away.'

Wilton didn't see any point in denying it.

'So?'

'Marshal Doyle came round asking me questions but I never said nothing but I reckon he'd be interested, don't you? 'Cos I reckon it means you shot that judge. Marshal might even give me some sorta reward. Or mebbe you could give me a reward of your own for keeping my mouth shut?' Turner's eyes glinted greedily.

They glinted even more when Wilton nodded.

'Yeah, maybe I could.'

Turner smiled. This was all going much better than he'd hoped. It was easy. The man was obviously scared of what he knew and what he might do with that knowledge.

'I reckon it'd be worth quite a bit, don't you? Keeping quiet?'

'Oh, yeah, I do.'

Good, good, Turner rubbed his hands together.

'Only thing is, I'm also wondering.'

'Wondering what?' Something suddenly appeared in the other man's face and voice so that for the first time Turner wasn't so sure of himself, hoped he hadn't made a mistake in coming here.

Wilton gave a small smirk.

'Well, Mr Turner, I can't help but wonder why you should believe that having committed one murder I wouldn't be only too willing to commit a second.'

CHAPTER EIGHT

Jubal Judd finished his cup of coffee in the hotel dining-room. Time to start work.

As he went out into the lobby, the snobbish clerk looked him up and down and just about forced himself to speak.

'A lovely day again today.'

It certainly was. The sun shone out of a clear blue sky and a breeze rustled through the pines in the nearby hills, making it pleasantly warm. Although it was still early the stores along Main Street were already open for business. Not many people were yet about but several women gossiped outside the dry-goods store opposite while a few horses were tied up at the hitching rail.

From somewhere across the street Judd caught the glimpse of the sun shining on a rifle barrel. Followed instantly by the loud crack of the weapon. And a bullet smashed into the rim of the hotel doorway above his head.

Judd flung himself to the ground. With more bullets following his every move, he covered his head with his arms and wriggled backwards. He heard someone scream. From across the way a horse whinnied and, pulling its reins free of the hitching post, galloped away down the street.

'What's going on?' the hotel clerk cried in fright. A bullet crashed through the window, breaking it in a shower of glass. Wisely the clerk asked no more questions but hid behind his desk.

Somehow Judd managed to dodge back into the hotel. He threw himself behind a tall aspidistra plant, another bullet sending several of its leaves cascading down around his shoulders. Kicking the door shut behind him, he drew his gun and peered out of the broken window. But there was nothing to see. No more shooting. He glanced across at the women opposite, who were huddled in the store doorway, and breathed a sigh of relief as he saw that none appeared to be hurt. He stood up, finding he was breathing heavily.

At the same time, the young deputy, Pat Fisher, came running into view, gun in his hand. He stopped outside the hotel, gaping at the smashed window before staring round. He was too late. The shooter had long gone.

'Are you all right?' Judd asked the clerk.

'I . . . I think so.' The man wiped his forehead with a handkerchief. 'But I have to tell you this is a respectable hotel. We're not used . . .'

Judd ignored the man's complaints and went outside to join Fisher.

Others, who had also taken cover, emerged more slowly to add their demands to the deputy's to know what the shooting was about. They were shocked. Ashby was usually a quiet town. This was the second shooting in a few days.

'It must have been Wilton,' Judd told Fisher.

'Did you see him?'

'No. He was in that alley over by the store. I saw the glint of his rifle . . .'

Which had saved his life. He was already ducking when the bullet struck the door above him. He would have been shot otherwise.

'. . . but he was well hidden. It was a good spot for an ambush.'

'Who's going to pay for this?' the hotel clerk demanded fussily, indicating the broken window.

'Bring it up at the next meeting of the town council,' Fisher said impatiently, causing the man to tut and mutter something about the lack of manners of the younger generation. 'Come on, Marshal, let's see if we can find anything.' He was obviously anxious to impress Judd.

Thinking they would be unlucky, Judd followed him through the gaping, excited crowd, taking no notice of the questions and comments. 'Where's Marshal Doyle?' he said, as they reached the mouth of the narrow alley.

'He had to go out early this morning.' Fisher holstered his gun as he saw the alley was empty. 'There was a report of some stolen cattle winding up on someone else's land. He said to tell you he'd be back as soon as he'd found them.'

'Look, this must be where Wilton was hiding.' Judd indicated the scuff marks in the earth close by

THE LONG DARK TRAIL

the wall of the store.

'Yeah but there ain't nothing else to see. The bastard seems good at vanishing.'

Judd nodded in agreement. He walked to the end of the short alley but it just led into another alley. Nothing there.

'He knows the town well. And he's clever enough to leave few traces behind.'

'Marshal, I don't think this is all.' Suddenly Fisher looked very worried. 'I was on my way to find you when I heard the shooting.'

'Why? What is it?'

'The livery is locked up and there ain't no sign of Old Roger. He's usually open early because he knows there're always cowboys up and about, waiting to return to their ranches. But he ain't there and I knew you and Marshal Doyle were going to speak to him today so I wondered if anything was wrong. . . .' His voice trailed away uncertainly.

'Was the livery open when Doyle rode out this morning?'

'I don't know. Both me and Mr Doyle keep our horses in the stables behind the jailhouse.'

'Are you sure Turner's not about?'

'Yes, sir. He's not home either 'cos I went and looked there. I didn't know what to do next. There's a group of cowboys hanging around the stables, wanting to get their horses. They've got a long ride in front of 'em.'

Judd wasn't worried about the cowboys' troubles, he was worried about Turner. He didn't like the sound of this.

'OK, let's go and see.'

When he and Fisher turned the corner to the business district they saw four or five young men hovering by the stable doors, looking both anxious and angry. With Fisher close behind him, Judd pushed through the group. He rattled the stable doors but they were securely locked. He tried to peer through any cracks in the wood. Like much else in Ashby, the stables were a fairly new construction and well made. He couldn't make out much but, although it could be his imagination, he thought he saw a shadow where there shouldn't be one.

'Pat, do you know if there's a spare key to these doors?' If not they'd have to break them open.

The young man frowned.

'I guess Mr Anderson at the dry-goods store might have one.'

Judd remembered Doyle saying Anderson was the leader of the town council.

'Go and see.'

Fisher paused. 'What is it? Is Old Roger sick? He drinks, you know.'

'Never mind that. Just get the key if you can.'

By now the clerk who worked for Wells Fargo had arrived to open up the office for the first stagecoach of the day. He wandered over.

'What's wrong?'

'Old Roger ain't here yet,' one of the cowboys complained. 'We want our horses. We've gotta get back.'

'Did you see him yesterday?' Judd asked the clerk.

'Only when I was on my way home,' the man

replied. 'He came to the door, looking mighty pleased with himself. I asked him why he looked so happy, which was unusual to say the least, and he said something about not being in this godforsaken place doing his godforsaken job much longer. When I said how come, he said he was getting some money from someone and leaving straight off.'

'Did he say who he was getting the money from?'

The clerk shook his head. 'But then I didn't ask him. To be honest I thought it was probably one of Old Roger's stories and I didn't take much notice. He either hardly says nothing or else he'll be gabbling on for hours. I could see he wanted to boast and tell tall tales so I didn't give him any encouragement. But,' another shake of his head, 'this isn't like him. Do you think he got the money last night and has left already? It would be just like him to leave everyone in the lurch.'

'No, I don't think he's left,' Judd said but didn't elaborate on what he meant.

Fisher arrived at a run with the key. Judd took it from him, unlocked the doors and pushed them back. Early-morning light flooded into the stables.

'Oh Christ!' the cowboy exclaimed, while the Wells Fargo clerk staggered back and was violently sick.

Roger Turner hung from one of the beams supporting the roof. His body swayed slightly in the breeze coming through the open doors. His eyes bulged and his tongue stuck out from his mouth.

Clearly, he was dead.

CHAPTER NINE

'Everyone keep back,' Judd ordered, somewhat unnecessarily as no one showed any inclination to approach the body. 'Pat, fetch Hicks.'

'Yes, sir.' Fisher was glad to hurry away.

'I can't believe it,' the clerk moaned after he'd recovered from being sick. 'I was only speaking to him yesterday and now the poor bastard's dead. Why the hell should he kill himself when he was so pleased with his good fortune?'

Judd didn't answer. He had no intention of discussing Turner's death with anyone but Doyle, and maybe Doctor Hicks.

'What about our horses?' the cowboy said.

'You'll get them once the doctor's examined the body,' Judd snapped. 'In the meantime show some respect.'

The cowboys withdrew slightly, muttering amongst themselves but not daring to argue. And the clerk, not wanting to be involved any more than necessary, said he'd have to open up for his customers and hurried away.

Judd went into the stables and stared round. This wasn't right, not right at all.

Immediately he arrived Doctor Hicks said:

'Best cut him down. There's nothing I can do for him.'

Together with a couple of the cowboys Fisher manhandled Turner down from the beam and laid him on the ground. Hicks bent to examine the body.

While he did so Judd turned to the deputy.

'Help these cowboys get their horses so they can be on their way.' At the moment they were in *his* way. 'Then once the undertaker has taken Turner's body away lock the place up again. I don't want people coming in here yet awhile.'

'Do you think—'

'I'm not thinking anything but I want Doyle to see exactly what's happened. Well?' Judd added to Hicks who had stood up.

'Death by strangulation,' Hicks confirmed. He frowned. 'But while it looks straightforward enough there are several bruises on his arms and a nasty one on his jaw which makes me wonder whether his death was self-inflicted.'

Judd was certain it wasn't.

'Or whether it was a killing.' Hicks's eyes were lit up with curiosity.

Knowing the man would likely start asking questions he didn't want to answer, Judd thanked him quickly and turned away. Rather huffily Hicks packed up his doctor's bag and left.

Judd decided that once Fisher returned with the undertaker he'd set him to ask questions of those few businessmen who had places down here. Find out if they'd seen or heard anything the day before. But he guessed this was an empty part of town at night and that most people, like the Wells Fargo clerk, had avoided Roger Turner. He didn't hold out a great deal of hope. Turner's house would have to be searched.

He would also send off a telegram to the United States Marshals' Service to ask for their help. If there was anything to find out about Rufus Wilton they would have it in their records. Of course if Wilton had made it a habit to keep changing his name it was unlikely there would be anything to find.

It was late morning when Simon Doyle rode back into Ashby. He was tired and annoyed, his clothes covered in a layer of dust. Judd was sitting in the marshal's office. He looked up as Doyle came in, rose to his feet and poured out coffee for them both.

Doyle slumped in his chair, taking off his hat and gratefully accepting the drink.

'What the hell is going on?' he demanded. 'I saw Pat outside. He told me you found Old Roger dead and that you were shot at. You ain't hurt, are you?' He didn't want anything to happen to a US marshal as well as a judge in his town.

Judd waved away the attack on him; it was part and parcel of his job. Quickly he told Doyle about Turner.

Doyle listened with growing concern.

'Hell!' was his muttered comment which seemed to Judd to sum up the situation. 'You think Wilton was responsible?'

'Who else? I want you to take a look at where and how we found Turner's body. See if you agree with me.'

'OK.' Doyle gulped down the rest of his coffee and with a little sigh got to his feet again.

'What about you?' Judd asked as they left the office.

'What about me, what?'

'Did you find the stolen cattle?'

'Hell, no!' Doyle said angrily. 'It proved a wild-goose chase. There were no damn cattle to be seen anywhere. I've been out wasting my time.'

'Who told you about them?'

'No one. I found a note left on my desk.'

'Who from?'

'I don't know. It wasn't signed. I thought it was from some cowboy who'd spotted the cattle in passing. When I didn't find them I thought he must've mistook the place. Or,' Doyle came to a sudden halt, 'do you think I was sent deliberately out of town?'

'Who knows?' Judd shrugged. 'It could have been a genuine mistake. Or Wilton could have wanted you out of the way while he shot at me and when Turner's body was found.' Who knew what went on in the mind of someone like Wilton?

At the stable quite a crowd had gathered in the road but Doyle ignored all their questions and followed Judd inside. They shut the door behind them so they wouldn't be disturbed.

'I suppose we were meant to think Turner committed suicide,' Doyle said once Judd had pointed out where and how the body had been found.

'If so it was a helluva clumsy effort.' Judd spread out his hands. 'For a start, where's whatever he stood on?'

'He could've tied the rope round his neck while supporting himself on the beam and then jumped.' Doyle sounded extremely doubtful.

'Maybe but that would have been difficult to say the least. Why not stand on a stool or a bucket, both easily found in a livery stable, then kick it away? I think Wilton murdered Turner and he doesn't care if we're not fooled by his set-up here. In fact, it's likely he wants us to realize the truth.'

'Why?'

'Because he's a foolhardy bastard who thinks he's cleverer than us.'

Doyle nodded in agreement. 'Do you think Old Roger was killed here? There ain't no sign of a struggle.'

'Isn't it more likely he went to see Wilton rather than Wilton coming here where he might not have found Turner alone?'

'And that Wilton killed him wherever they met and then brought him back here?'

'That'd be my guess. He wouldn't want to force Turner to walk through the streets at gunpoint and risk him getting away.'

'No.' Doyle paused and frowned. 'But if so it meant he'd have to find a way of carrying the body through the streets.'

'I know.'

'And, hell, that means Wilton doesn't care if he

was seen or, hell, that he was willing to kill anyone else who did see them.'

'He's mocking us, Simon.' Judd was angry. 'Even worse he's mocking the law.'

'And why kill Old Roger?'

'According to the Wells Fargo clerk Turner was boasting about getting money from someone. Enough to leave town. Don't you think it's likely that Turner did see the judge's killer like you thought he had and decided he'd try a spot of blackmail? Instead he got himself killed.'

'Hell, yes! That would be just like Old Roger. He was a greedy bastard.' Doyle sighed. 'Even so! He might've been a cantankerous bugger but he didn't deserve to end up being murdered. What now?'

'I'm not sure. Perhaps I might visit the Carmichaels, learn about the robbery they had there, but that'll have to be after Miss Geddings arrives. I should be here to meet her.'

'I doubt the Carmichaels will be able to tell you much but it's worth a try.'

'What about you?'

'I'd better go and have a word with Mr Anderson. See what he and the town council want to do about the stables. Someone will have to be employed to run them.' Doyle didn't sound as if he relished the idea.

Rufus Wilton watched all the comings and goings with a hidden grin. It would never do to grin when everyone was so damn serious and upset. Everything was proving such splendid fun. The only annoying thing was his failure to kill Jubal Judd. He'd made a mistake there. But still, and this time he couldn't prevent himself from grinning, he could always try again.

CHAPTER TEN

Judd sat in the café, drinking coffee and eating a huge slab of apple pie when Pat Fisher came to find him.

'Mr Judd,' Fisher said, 'Mr Doyle sent me for you. Miss Geddings has arrived.'

'Good.' Judd stood up. 'Where is she?'

'At the Planter's Hotel.'

As they walked out into the street, Judd said:

'By the way, Pat, how are you getting on questioning those who work round the livery stable?'

Fisher grimaced. 'I've got a couple more people to talk to but so far no one has seen or heard anything.'

Just what Judd had expected.

'OK, I'll see you later.'

Not for Barbara Geddings the hotel where Judd was staying. Like her father before her, she had booked rooms at the best and dearest hotel Ashby had to offer, where only the wealthy could afford to stay. It was situated all by itself out on the road above the river. Here it was quiet, the only sounds that of birds singing and the water far below as it ran between its high rocky banks. From the building would be a view of the river too, down through the pine trees. Even on the hottest of summer days the air would be fresh and clean.

A high wall surrounded the property, which looked more like a house than a hotel, being two storeys high with an enclosed porch at the front and a turret decorating one corner.

Very nice too, Judd thought.

He was shown into the parlour at the rear of the hotel. In deference to the judge's death and Barbara's arrival, the shades had been pulled across the windows making the room dark and stuffy. Two oil-lamps were lit against the gloom.

By their light Judd saw two women sitting in comfortable armchairs on either side of a fireplace. Marshal Doyle stood in the middle of the room, twisting his hat round and round in his hands, looking tongue-tied and most uncomfortable in their presence. Not surprisingly, both Reverend Stroud and Doctor Hicks were also there.

Judd decided that both men must be keeping a watch on the stagecoaches to see who was coming and going; Hicks because he was nosy and Stroud because he didn't want the doctor to learn something before he did, although maybe knowing Miss Geddings was due to arrive today he had been keeping a watch out for her.

'Marshal,' Doyle said, 'this is Miss Barbara Geddings and her housekeeper, Mrs Nora Wood.'

Both women looked tired and Barbara had a handkerchief clutched in one hand. She had changed from her travelling-clothes into a black dress decorated with jet beads across the bodice.

'Marshal Judd, pleased to meet you,' Barbara said, as Judd shook her hand. 'Perhaps you can tell me what has been done to catch my father's murderer.'

She glanced at Doyle, who obviously had been so overawed by meeting a pretty and rich young lady he hadn't been able to say much of anything to her.

Unlike Doyle, Judd was used to dealing with all sorts of people in all sorts of situations.

'Miss Geddings, first let me say I'm sorry about your father.'

'Thank you. I still can't believe it.' Barbara dabbed at her eyes with the handkerchief.

Hicks took her other hand. 'If it's any comfort to you, your father wouldn't have suffered,' he said. 'His death was very quick and he would hardly have had time to realize what was happening.'

'Thank you.' Barbara gave him a weak smile.

'Miss Geddings,' Judd went on, 'did you know your father summoned me here to see him?'

'Really?' Barbara's eyes widened. 'I can't think—'

'Is there any need to bother Miss Geddings with all this right now?' Reverend Stroud interrupted sounding angry. 'She is naturally extremely upset and has endured a long journey. I'm sure she would appreciate being left alone for a while with her grief.'

'No, no, it's all right,' Barbara said. 'Please, sit down all of you.'

'Are you sure?' Stroud asked.

'Yes. I want to know. Thank you though for your concern. Nora, would you please summon a waiter and ask him to bring coffee for us all? I'm sure these gentlemen would appreciate it.'

'Yeah, thanks, we would,' Doyle said. He sounded as if he could do with something far stronger than coffee.

'So, Mr Judd, what did my father want?'

'I don't think I can do any better than show you the letter he sent me.'

Barbara read the letter to herself, hand holding the handkerchief to her mouth as she did so, then out loud to Nora, who looked as puzzled as Barbara.

'I don't understand. Who is this man my father saw?'

'That's what we all want to know,' Doyle muttered grimly.

'Is he the one who shot my father?'

'Yes,' Judd said. 'Can you or Mrs Wood help us to identify him?'

'No, I'm sorry,' Barbara said, while Nora shook her head.

Judd, realizing he had been hoping Barbara could tell him something useful, clamped down on a feeling of disappointment. He took back the letter and put it in his pocket.

'The judge never spoke to you about Rufus Wilton?' he asked.

Barbara sighed. 'No, Mr Judd, I wish he had. But if the trial was, what, fourteen years ago, I would only have been seven or eight. When I was young he never told me anything about his work. In fact, he seldom spoke to me about the trials he held even once I was grown up.'

'Nor to me or Mrs Geddings,' Nora added. 'He didn't think it right to discuss in the home the lawbreakers he came up against in his work.'

'It was obviously an important trial, one he would have remembered; did he never mention Wilton later on?'

'Marshal,' Stroud intervened, 'Miss Geddings has already said she doesn't know this man.'

Barbara waved a hand towards the reverend.

'Mr Judd is only doing his job. I don't mind, really.'

Judd, who didn't like being told what to do, kept his temper with some difficulty.

'I suppose you have none of his papers?'

'No, he kept everything with him. He wrote notes on practically everything he did because he intended to use them to write a history of the frontier. Have you found them?'

'Yes, they were in his room here at the hotel. Someone is going through them now.'

'Thank goodness. I wouldn't like to think of them being lost. Mr Judd, have neither you nor Marshal Doyle found anything to say whom this Wilton is masquerading as now?'

'No,' Doyle said.

'Not yet,' Judd added.

'Oh dear. It's so difficult to take in.'

'This has all been an ordeal for Miss Geddings,' Stroud tried again. 'I really think she should be left alone for a while. She needs to rest. And, Miss Geddings, we also have to discuss the funeral arrangements.'

'Of course.'

'You've decided to bury your father here then?' Judd said.

'Yes. It was a hard decision especially as mother's grave is in Tucson. But Tucson was never really home to Father. Whereas he evidently told Doctor Hicks that he liked Ashby enough to want to retire here.'

'Yes, he did.' Hicks sounded important, as if he had been privy to the judge's secrets.

'I think it's a good idea,' Stroud added. 'I'm sure it's something he would want.'

He and Hicks scowled at one another, both wanting to take credit for knowing what the judge had intended to do.

Judd could think of nothing further to ask Barbara. He nodded at Doyle, who stood up.

'You have our sympathy, Miss Geddings, and you may be sure we're doing our best to find your father's killer.'

'Thank you.'

'She's a nice young lady,' Judd said as he and Doyle left the hotel.

'Yeah, very.'

Judd hid a smile. From Doyle's flushed face and adoring tone it was clear he found Miss Barbara Geddings very attractive. But whether he would ever find the courage to tell her so was another matter altogether.

CHAPTER ELEVEN

Judd saddled and bridled one of the horses Doyle pointed out was kept for hire, choosing a mare that looked to have plenty of stamina. Not that the Carmichaels lived far away but he wanted to be there and back before nightfall. The way took him along by the river. It was a pleasant ride for a breeze came from the water, which ran fast and strong, and trees grew close to the riverbank, providing welcome shade. As he rode along he realized this was good country with plentiful grass, suitable for both ranching and farming.

The Carmichael ranch was easy to find, situated not far from the river. It was small and perhaps ranch was too grand a name for it, for while it supported a number of cattle there was also a field of vegetables divided into strips growing pumpkins, melons and potatoes. The house was just a wooden shack surrounded by a shed, the beginnings of a barn and an empty pole corral.

As he rode up a large dog of indeterminate breed came out to greet him, barking as he dodged under the mare's hoofs but wagging his tail as well so that when Judd dismounted he had no fear of attack. At the same time Mrs Carmichael came to stand in the doorway. Understandably she looked nervous and Judd didn't miss the fact that she had placed a shotgun within easy reach. She was in her early thirties, a short plump woman with brown hair caught up in an untidy bun and a face burnt brown by the sun.

'Mrs Carmichael?'

Her eyes screwed up as she wondered how he, a stranger, knew her.

'That's right. My husband isn't far away.'

Her husband could be anywhere. There was no sign of him working in the field.

'Come here, Rascal.' She called the dog to her side.

'It's all right.' Judd didn't want her to be worried. 'I'm here on behalf of Marshal Doyle. I'm a United States marshal. My name's Jubal Judd.' He made sure she could see his badge of office.

She looked surprised, obviously wondering why someone as grand as a US marshal should be calling on her.

'You may have heard about the murder of Judge Geddings?'

She nodded. News travelled fast in places like Ashby.

'What's that to do with us?'

'It's a long story. I'd like to talk to you about the robbery you suffered.'

'Surely that was drifters.'

'Maybe, but we think it might be connected.'

Mrs Carmichael made up her mind.

'You'd better come in.'

She opened the door wider and pushed the dog out of the way. At the same time she picked up the shotgun, not about to take any chances. She led the way through the shack's main room to a tiny, cool kitchen at the back. A door opened on to the yard, where some chickens pecked in the dirt. Everything in the house was neat and tidy. And the furniture, although home-made, was substantial.

'Sit down.' She indicated a chair at the table in the middle of the room. 'Would you like some lemon-ade? Coffee?'

'Lemonade would be nice.'

As she poured out two glasses the dog sat down in the open doorway and after a moment lay down with his head on his paws.

'Why has Marshal Doyle changed his mind?' Mrs Carmichael joined Judd at the table. 'He was sure it was drifters. Kids probably on their way to become cowboys.'

'The judge was killed by someone he'd known a long while ago who was a thief. And it's possible the same person robbed you.'

'Oh, I see. Who?'

'That's what we don't know. Mrs Carmichael, what happened?'

'It was horrible,' she said with a little shudder. 'It felt like our place had been violated.'

'I understand neither you nor your husband was here.'

'No, we weren't, thank goodness. It was the first

Monday in the month and that's when Eddie and me always go into Ashby. To buy supplies and sell whatever we've managed to grow.'

'Always?'

'Yes.'

Which wouldn't be hard for anyone living in Ashby to find out.

'We got home in the evening . . . and, oh my, the shock!' The woman's hands went to her heart as they must have done that day when she and her husband realized they'd been robbed. 'It wasn't so much what was stolen, though that was bad enough, it was the damage done. It still upsets me to think about what happened, though Eddie says I must put it behind me and forget it.' She sighed. 'It's hard to do that.'

'How did the thief get in?'

'Through the window in our bedroom. The shutters were completely smashed.'

'What about your dog?'

Mrs Carmichael looked fondly at the animal.

'We take him into town with us. I couldn't have borne it if anything had happened to Rascal.' Tears came into her eyes. Looking embarrassed she quickly wiped them away and jumped up to pour them out more lemonade. 'It was such a shock. There was no warning outside.'

'You didn't notice the window?'

She shook her head. 'No, not until later, because it's at the back of the house. But, of course, directly we opened the front door . . .' She broke off, sighed and with another shudder went on: 'Oh, Marshal Judd, everything was in such a mess. Cushions and bed-linen had been flung into the middle of the room and some of it was slashed and torn. My few pieces of good china were smashed. A small mirror broken. It was as if someone had gone on a rampage.'

That was obviously what had made Doyle think it was drifters, wild boys, who were responsible.

'When Marshal Doyle came out to us he said it looked as if the damage that had been done was more important to the thieves than what they'd stolen.'

'Did he find any evidence that more than one person was responsible?'

'I don't think so. He just thought that because so much damage had been done.'

'What was stolen?' Judd finished his lemonade.

'Nothing of monetary value. Look around you, Marshal Judd, we're not well-off people. Just small-time ranchers trying our best. We haven't got a lot to steal. But a few odd coins left on the table by the door had disappeared. An ornament. And . . .'

'And?'

'A ring Eddie had bought for me soon after we met.' Mrs Carmichael had tears in her eyes again. 'It wasn't worth a great deal but it had a great senti-mental value and it can never be replaced.'

'Who would have known that?'

'You think it was taken on purpose?'

'I don't know, maybe,' Judd said with a shrug.

Still tearful Mrs Carmichael said: 'I guess most people knew how much my ring meant to me. I never made any secret of it. In fact I suppose I boasted about it. And now I'll never see it again.' She began to sob.

'It's not your fault,' Judd said, patting her shoulder. 'It's the fault of whoever stole it. You mustn't blame yourself.'

As he rode away, Judd thought about what he'd learned. Not much. Not anything to prove it was Rufus Wilton who'd committed the robbery rather than drifters, although he was sure Wilton was responsible. Nor, more important, anything to prove Wilton's identity.

He thought the Carmichaels were lucky they hadn't been home when the thief came to call. That the next family might not be so fortunate.

Although he didn't like to admit it even to himself, he was unsettled by what he'd found out. By the senseless vindictiveness of it. Over the years he'd had to deal with all types: stagecoach robbers, army deserters, murderers. Some were vicious, some stupid, others destined to spend most of their lives in jail. They were usually uncomplicated. Their motives – greed, laziness, even hate – easy to understand and deal with.

Rufus Wilton and his motives were something else.

Judd knew he was good enough with his guns, being both fast and accurate, to rely on them in almost any situation. Had, in fact, been involved in several gunfights from which he'd emerged as victor. Remained cool in deadly confrontations.

But for the first time in his life he had doubts about whether he was good enough to handle this situation. He thought he might be afraid and he didn't like the feeling because since becoming a lawman he couldn't remember being afraid of anything or anyone.

He thought the sooner the man was caught and stopped the better it would be.

CHAPTER TWELVE

'I believe this would make an ideal spot for the grave, don't you, Miss Geddings?' Reverend Stroud stopped by the low wall that surrounded the dusty cemetery. Nearby was one of the pine trees that shaded the ground, the breeze blowing through its branches.

'Yes, it's beautiful,' Barbara agreed. 'Father can be at rest here.'

She glanced about her. It was late afternoon, becoming cooler now the sun was going down, shadows lengthening. Saint Anne's stood at the bottom of a high hill, which was covered in trees and bushes, while bright flowers grew thickly in grassy patches. The church was a large building, painted white with a bell-tower at the front and ornately carved wooden doors. When Stroud had shown her round inside, it had been cool and dim. A place of peace and quiet where Barbara had immediately felt at home.

'If you agree, Miss Geddings, I think your father should be buried as soon as possible. I can make all the arrangements for you if you like.'

'Yes, please, if you would.' Tears came into

Barbara's eyes. She didn't feel up to dealing with everything herself, dealing with strangers. 'It's nice of you to take so much trouble.'

'Believe me it's no trouble.' Stroud placed a hand on her arm. 'I'm so sorry about what happened. I didn't know your father, the judge, but from all I heard of him he was a fine man.'

'Yes he was.' Barbara sighed. A fine man, a fine judge, but never much of a family man.

Stroud leant against the wall, looking up the hill.

'Have you any idea of what you'll do now? I mean, will you remain here, as your father appeared to want, or go back home to Tucson?'

'I'm not sure.' Barbara frowned. 'This has been such a shock. I haven't taken it in yet. I certainly haven't had time or inclination to make any decisions about my future.'

'Of course. Of course. I don't mean to press you.' Stroud ran a hand through his beard.

'Father liked it here but I don't know anyone—'

'It's a very friendly town. I'm a stranger myself but everyone has made me very welcome.'

'And mother is buried in Tucson.'

'It's quite a problem. You wouldn't consider returning to New York?'

'Oh no. I would be even more of a stranger there than in Ashby.'

'You've never been back?'

'No.' Barbara gave a little smile. 'And nor did my parents.' Her mother had wanted to but her father never had, making her realize, yet again, how more like her father than her mother she was.

86

'I'm sure that whatever decision you make will be the right one. Will Mrs Wood stay with you?'

'I hope so.'

'You're lucky to have her with you now to help you.'

'That I am. I don't know what I'd do without her.'

'I hope you also know I'm here to help as well.'

'Thank you.' Barbara blushed a little.

'And if you need to talk, to discuss anything, seek advice, well, please don't hesitate to call on me, my door is always open.' Stroud pointed to a small, neat house, half-hidden by the church.

'Thank you,' Barbara repeated. 'You'll let me know once you've made the arrangements, won't you?'

'Of course.'

'I'd better be getting on back, Nora will be wondering where I am.'

'I'll walk with you to the hotel.'

'No, there's no need, I'll be all right.'

Stroud took her arm. 'With everything that is going on in the town you must take care.'

'You think I'm in danger?' Barbara sounded startled.

'Not once this Wilton learns you know nothing about him, no. Until then . . .' Stroud shrugged. 'Yes, I'm afraid you and Mrs Wood could be in danger.'

'Oh dear.' As they headed down the slope of the hill to the cemetery gates, Barbara added: 'I suppose you have no idea who this Wilton could be?'

Stroud frowned.

'You do, don't you?' Barbara came to a halt, facing him.

'Oh no, no, I can't say I know, no.'

'But?' As Stroud paused, Barbara added quite angrily, 'You can't keep quiet about something like this.'

Stroud glanced up at his church as if seeking inspiration.

'Well, Miss Geddings,' he went on reluctantly, 'it does seem to me that Doctor Hicks is often missing from town, and no one knows where he's gone or what he's doing.'

Barbara looked shocked, as if that was the last thing she'd expected.

'Surely that's to do with his doctoring?'

'Oh yes, of course, sometimes. But as far as I can make out no one seems to know where he comes from or anything about his background. And it seems strange for a doctor to bury himself in a small place like Ashby.' Barbara frowned and he added: 'You don't believe it possible?'

'Well, no, I don't. How could someone like Wilton, a thief, indeed how could anyone, pretend to be a doctor? Surely their lack of skill would soon be found out?'

Stroud frowned as well. 'There is that, of course, and Hicks does appear to be good at what he does. But then how many people out here have much knowledge of doctoring? Hicks could be fooling everyone. Getting by with luck on his side. After all, as well as dangerous Wilton must also be extremely clever to have eluded capture in all this time. Must behave in a way we can't possibly understand.'

'I suppose so.' Barbara brushed a lock of hair from

her face, looking both anxious and a little scared.

'And I really cannot think of anyone else that it might be.'

'How long has Hicks been doctor here, do you know?'

'I think he arrived some two or three years ago. Soon after the town began to grow.' Stroud took her hand for a moment. 'I hope I haven't upset you?'

'Oh no.' But he had. It was all very disquieting. She paused. 'Have you discussed this with Marshal Judd? Or Marshal Doyle?'

'Why no, no I haven't. Do you think I should?'

'Yes. Don't you? Supposing you're right?'

A look of dismay crossed Stroud's face.

'Oh dear, I don't want to cause trouble for anyone. And, of course, I have no evidence . . . perhaps I shouldn't have said anything. I really don't know. . . .'

But Barbara did. She decided that even if Reverend Stroud wouldn't mention his suspicions to either lawman then she would do so. Whether the man was right or wrong, and she still thought he must be wrong, they ought to know because it might help them discover the truth.

CHAPTER THIRTEEN

The funeral of Judge Geddings was held the next day at 11 o'clock in the morning.

It seemed the whole town came to a respectful halt for it. Every store along Main Street was closed and bystanders lined the sidewalks, men with bared heads, women in black, children hushed and quiet.

Old Roger Turner's funeral had been held the day before, but hardly anyone had bothered to attend that. He hadn't been liked and the suspicion that he'd committed suicide kept people away. This was completely different. None had met Judge Geddings but each knew of his reputation. Knew what he'd done to bring law and order to the frontier, making people's lives that little bit safer. Besides it was a break from routine and wondering who had shot him provided something different to talk about.

The undertaker polished his hearse until it shone brightly in the sun, the black horse had black feathers fixed in its harness. A black-suited boy, the undertaker's son, beat mournfully on a drum and marched in front of the hearse as it made a slow way towards the church.

Barbara followed behind supported by Nora. Everyone thought the judge's daughter very brave for the dignified way in which she conducted herself. Then came Marshal Judd and Simon Doyle with Doctor Hicks and the other members of the town council.

Reverend Stroud waited at the church door to meet the coffin. He led the way inside, the mourners following on behind. As they took their seats he stepped forward to conduct the service. Prayers were said, hymns sung and Stroud spoke about the judge's life.

When he intoned: 'It is a sad day for us all when a good man like Judge Geddings can be struck down for doing his duty,' Barbara began to cry. Nora put a comforting arm round her, wiping her own eyes.

'Do you think the killer is here?' Doyle whispered, having seen Judd staring at the mourners.

'I wouldn't be at all surprised. Laughing at us, I expect.'

The question was who? He certainly wasn't giving himself away.

But Rufus Wilton was there all right. He watched everyone, laughing inside at their expressions of anger, pity and sorrow. He raised his hand to his mouth, hiding a smile. If only they knew! But, of course, how could they know? He was much too intelligent for any of them.

After the service everyone walked out to the newly dug grave, where the funeral was concluded.

Once it was over Doyle went off to help Fisher make sure there was no trouble and everybody went about their business. He was also anxious to avoid John Proctor who, earlier on, had been in earnest conversation with the rest of the town council and who wouldn't hesitate to give the marshal a lecture even at such a solemn occasion.

Judd remained behind, wanting to pay his respects to Barbara. He waited until the other mourners had done the same. For a while Reverend Stroud remained close by her side, shaking people's hands, helping Nora to support her. Then with a comforting word to her he went over to supervise the filling-in of the grave. Soon the only one remaining by her side, besides Nora, was David Marston.

'Miss Geddings,' Judd said, raising his Stetson. 'How are you?'

'Oh, Marshal.' Barbara acknowledged him with a wan smile. 'Thank you for attending. It was a fine service in a lovely setting. Mr Stroud said such nice things about my father. And now Mr Marston has been telling me how he met my father when he arrived in Ashby.'

'And how much I wish I could have gotten to know him better,' Marston said with a nod. 'Marshal Judd, I was on my way to see you and Mr Doyle,' he added, looking quite pleased with himself.

'Oh? Have you found something helpful amongst the judge's papers?'

'No, but I have been busy making enquiries of other courts in Arizona. And I've found out where the judge was sitting fourteen years ago when he tried Rufus Wilton!'

'Oh, that's good news, isn't it?' Nora said to Barbara.

'You have?' Judd hoped something was going his way at last.

'Yes. It was a place called Juniper Creek. That's down near the border.'

Barbara nodded eagerly.

'I remember Father going there. Not fourteen years ago but several times recently. Do you remember, Nora, he said how much the place had changed, except that it was still pretty lawless.'

'Shall I ask them to send us any papers they've got on the trial?' Marston asked.

'That could take time and the papers might not tell us much,' Judd said. 'Waiting for them' – and doing nothing meanwhile – 'could be a waste of time.'

He was only too well aware that the taking and writing-up of notes was not always as thorough as it should be, not even now, let alone fourteen years ago in a wild frontier town.

'How far away is Juniper Creek? How long would it take me to ride there?'

'A couple of days.' Marston hazarded a guess.

'It's a long way,' Barbara said.

'It might be best though. Who knows, there might be people still living there who remember both trial and Wilton and could fill in some of the background.'

'Oh, yes, I see, that's possible.'

'When will you go?' Marston asked.

'As soon as possible. Tomorrow probably. I'll need to see about some supplies first. Well done, Mr Marston.'

'Yes indeed,' Barbara added, making the man blush with pleasure.

'Mr Marston,' Nora said, 'would you care to come back to the hotel? They've provided a funeral feast. Reverend,' she turned to where Stroud hovered close by, 'will you come as well?'

'Of course, I'd be delighted.'

'Mr Judd?'

'I need to see Doyle first.'

Judd was about to leave when Barbara stopped him.

'Mr Judd, I must speak to you.' She caught hold of his arm, leading him away from where they could be overheard.

'What is it?'

'It's something Reverend Stroud mentioned to me yesterday. It might not mean anything but I think you should know. It's about Doctor Hicks.'

CHAPTER FOURTEEN

Rufus Wilton made up his mind. He would have to leave Ashby soon. After what he'd heard he knew it was too damn dangerous to stay much longer. While it was annoying it was just one of those things but surely, oh surely, he could afford to wait a little longer yet, do all those things he wanted to do first.

Like rob the Proctors. They were in town attending Geddings's funeral and, being so mean, rather than make another journey they'd probably stop to buy their monthly supplies at the same time. And John Proctor would doubtless want to talk to Marshal Doyle, demanding to know what he was doing to catch the killer, throwing his weight around. Stupid fool.

Wilton knew he was taking a chance in leaving town now with so many people about but it might be his only opportunity. In the event it proved easy to find the right time when most people had left the funeral feast and easier still to come up with a good excuse to slip away. He'd always been able to fool people, they were so willing to believe whatever they were told, to see the best in others. Idiots!

If he hurried he could reach the ranch and be back before the Proctors arrived home or anyone noted his absence.

He saddled his horse and keeping to the alleyways rode out of town. His usual cunning held and no one saw him. He didn't cross the river by the bridge where he might be spotted but rode further along and crossed it at the nearest ford. Sometimes the ford was dangerous but it was rarely impassable and today, after a short dry spell, it was neither. Once on the other side he put spurs to the horse's sides, setting it into a gallop, heading for the rangeland.

Galloping all the way it didn't take Wilton long to reach the Proctor ranch. As he'd expected, the place was quiet. Empty. He ignored the outbuildings, making straight for the rambling house which stood a little way away at the bottom of a hill.

The door was locked but he broke in without any difficulty. Immediately his greedy eyes lit upon a number of things his greedy heart wanted to steal but he pushed his feelings aside: he was here for money and only money for that couldn't be traced. And because he wanted to punish the Proctors, to do as much damage as he could.

As he made his way through the rooms he flung things around, smashing furniture, breaking glasses, stamping on the boys' few toys. As usual he began quite calmly, knowing what he was doing, but gradually he became more and more wild and excited. Out of control. On this occasion his wildness was fuelled by fury when he didn't find the fortune he hoped would be kept under the Proctors' bed.

He felt cheated, wronged, and no one did that to him without being paid back.

So furious was he, so intent on destroying every-thing that could be destroyed, he didn't hear the wagon being driven up to the house. Didn't hear it stop, nor the exclamations at the broken front door.

Didn't hear anything until there came a man's gasp and a woman's scream.

Arms raised aloft where he held a painting he was about to bring down on his knee, Wilton swung round. Standing in the doorway to the parlour was Proctor, a look of bewildered anger on his face, while behind him Alice and the two boys huddled together. Wilton grinned, amused by their helpless fear, their uncertainty at what they saw, as if they couldn't believe the evidence of their own eyes.

'What are you doing here?' Proctor demanded. 'What the hell do you think you're doing?'

'Well, Mr Proctor,' said Wilton, 'I was gonna rob you but it seems you don't have nothing worth goddamn stealing. So now I'll have to kill you instead.'

In the hotel's parlour, Nora poured coffee for her and Barbara.

'Here you are, dear.'

Barbara took the cup and smiled and sighed.

'Thank goodness everyone has gone,' she said. 'I thought they never would.'

'You can relax now. The worst part is over. You can now grieve alone and come to terms with your loss.'

Barbara nodded.

'And perhaps we can be on our way home.' Nora paused as she saw the look on the girl's face. 'Barbara, we are going back to Tucson soon aren't we?'

'It's just . . . I want, no need, to know who shot my father. I really can't just up and run away before then. It wouldn't be right. I'd understand if you decided you wanted to go back without me.' Barbara put down her cup of coffee and stared anxiously at the other woman, hoping she wouldn't do so.

'Don't be silly. It's just that if Reverend Stroud is right about how we might be in danger, surely we'd be safer in Tucson.'

'Oh, Nora, I know, but this Wilton must realize by now that neither of us can identify him. Nora . . . Nora, would you mind if I did decide to live here? Would you move here with me?'

'Of course I would.' Nora stood up, went over to the window and stared out at the trees and at the glimpse of river below. 'I think it's a lovely town. And it wouldn't be nearly so hot in summer as it is in Tucson.'

'At the same time we might get bad winters which we don't have in the desert!' Barbara laughed. 'Nowhere's perfect, is it?'

'Have you made up your mind to stay?'

'Oh no! No, I've had too many other things to think about. But Father did like it here and Reverend Stroud says it's a good, friendly town and will be even better if this Wilton is caught.'

'If? Doesn't he think he will be?'

'He has his doubts. Especially where Marshal Doyle is concerned.'

'I thought the marshal was doing his best. And he seems nice enough. He's a bit shy around young ladies like you that's all. It made him tongue-tied and awkward. I'm sure that's no reflection on his ability to do his job.'

Barbara said nothing to that.

'Anyway I can't see Marshal Judd letting anyone escape his grasp.'

'Nor can I,' Barbara admitted with a smile. After she finished her coffee she returned to the possibility of living in Ashby. 'Mr Stroud has offered to go to the real estate office with me. Discuss prices. He said he'd also help me look at suitable properties.'

'You like him, Mr Stroud I mean, don't you?'

Barbara reddened. 'He's been very helpful. And kind.'

'Well, don't let him press or persuade you into doing something you might regret.'

'I won't. Oh, Nora, don't worry.' Barbara went over to the woman, putting her arms around her. 'You know me. I can make up my own mind easily enough.'

'Yes, sometimes far too easily,' Nora scolded.

'That's true. But at least I don't need anyone doing it for me. And despite what you, and Mr Stroud, might think I really haven't made any decisions yet.'

Doctor Hicks was not best pleased. He'd had to leave town with everything that was going on there to deliver a baby. Thank goodness he'd been able to remain for the funeral but goodness only knew what he had missed at the funeral feast where he might have picked up all sorts of gossip.

It was Mrs Fellowes's ninth baby, you'd have thought she and her husband would know what to do by now. But no, Fellowes had ridden into Ashby and begged the doctor's help. And what could Hicks do but ride back with him?

At least the delivery had been easy and quick. Mother and daughter were both well. And as they didn't live far away he wouldn't be away long.

As Hicks drove the buggy along the top of the ridge he glanced down at the Proctor ranch. Their wagon was pulled up outside the house. Which meant they were home from Ashby, where he had met them earlier in the day. He looked at his watch. Just gone three o'clock. He still had six miles to go. Perhaps it would be best to break his journey. Have a cup of coffee with Proctor and a piece of Alice's delicious apple pie. Learn if anything had been decided by the town council.

He turned the horse's head and drove down to the ranch house. No one came out to greet him, which was unusual as one of the boys normally ran out to say hallo. He saw that not only was the wagon still loaded with supplies but the horse looked restless as if it had been waiting for a while.

And the front door was gaping open.

'Proctor!' he called. No reply.

He was sure something was wrong. Proctor would hardly leave the door open or the supplies unloaded. There was no sign of anyone in the yard. A little apprehensively he climbed down from the buggy and approached the house, pushing at the door, which he now saw had broken hinges.

'Proctor. You home?'

He walked down the hall. Everything was very quiet except for a strange buzzing noise coming from the parlour. He looked in. A cloud of flies rose up from the floor. Revealing what lay there.

'Oh my God!' Hicks gasped. 'Oh, God!'

He stumbled out of the house and paused for a moment to gain his breath. Then sobbing with fear and horror he clambered back into the buggy and sent the horse hell for leather back to Ashby.

CHAPTER FIFTEEN

'Murder! Murder!' Shouting out the word, Doctor Hicks drove the buggy fast down Main Street. By the time he reached the marshal's office, a great number of people had come out of stores and houses to see what had caused their normally neat and tidy doctor to be wild-eyed and covered with as much sweat as his horse.

Dragging the animal to a stop, Hicks rushed inside. Panting for breath, he leaned against the deputy's desk.

'Killed!' he managed to gasp. He pointed out of the door. 'The Proctors! All dead!'

Raising his eyebrows, Doyle glanced at Judd and hurried round to support the doctor.

'Take it easy, Doc. Pat, get Doctor Hicks a glass of water. Now, what is it? What's wrong?'

Hicks gulped down the water and wiped his forehead.

'John Proctor. His whole family. They've been murdered.'

'Christ,' Judd muttered while Doyle looked

stunned as if he was wondering what else could possibly happen.

'Here, Doc, sit down.' Fisher pulled out a chair and Hicks collapsed into it.

'Are you sure?' Doyle asked.

'Think I don't know a dead body when I see it?' Hicks snapped. Then his face crumpled. 'There was blood everywhere,' he said, almost in tears. 'Flies. God, I've never seen anything like it. Those poor people. I'm sorry.' He put his head in his hands and it was obvious they wouldn't get anything more out of him for a long while.

Judd took charge. He stood up and reached for his hat.

'We'd better go on out there. C'mon, Simon.'

'I thought you were getting ready to ride to Juniper Creek?'

'That can wait.'

'Yeah, yeah, I guess so. Pat, you stay here. Make sure the doctor gets home. Give him some whiskey or something. Clear the streets.'

'OK, Marshal.'

'I don't know how long we'll be.'

'How far to the Proctors?' Judd asked as they set out.

'Not far. 'Bout six miles. Jesus, I can't believe it. I only hope Hicks is wrong.'

It was quickly obvious that Hicks wasn't wrong, that he was only too right.

The bodies lay in a heap on the parlour floor. Blood surrounded them, was sprayed up the walls, over the furniture and the wreckage that was the rest of their belongings.

'Oh, dear God,' Doyle breathed in either a curse or a prayer.

While he stayed by the door, leaning against the wall as if his legs wouldn't support him, Judd ventured further into the room. He attempted to brush aside the flies that rose up in an angrily buzzing cloud at being disturbed. Clamping down hard on the sick feeling twisting his stomach, he stared at the four bodies.

John Proctor had been the first to be shot. In the stomach so, while not killed outright, he could do nothing to prevent what then happened to his wife and two sons. Not that they had been shot or killed quickly. All three had taken an awfully long time to die.

Judd glanced round the room. Three chairs faced each other in one corner. It was clear they wouldn't normally be placed like that. He thought Mrs Proctor and the two boys had been tied in the chairs so they would have to look at one another while they were tortured. And Proctor had lain, helplessly on the floor, watching as well, while they could hear his dying gasps. Eventually another bullet had put an end to the man's suffering.

When all four were dead their killer had arranged them in an ungainly pile in the middle of the room and left them to the flies.

'Oh God,' Doyle repeated. With an effort he pushed away from the door and came to stand by Judd. 'You know, all the way out here I sorta hoped that if the Proctors were dead, that they'd been killed by a couple of outlaws who just happened to ride by or even a bunch of renegade Indians.' The man gave a hollow laugh. 'Not that there's been any Indian trouble around Ashby for years. But I hoped. I also hoped their deaths were painless. That they would've known little about it. God, how wrong could I be.'

Judd didn't know what to say, so he said nothing.

Doyle turned to look at him.

'It was that sonofabitch, Wilton, wasn't it?'

'Look at the rest of the place. It's ransacked. My guess is Wilton was out here robbing the Proctors—'

'There are, were, rumours about Proctor having money hidden somewhere.'

'And they came back and caught him at it. They then had to be killed so they couldn't identify him.'

'But to kill them like this? To enjoy it. What sort of man would behave that way?' Doyle shook his head. 'It's beyond me.'

It was also beyond Judd but he didn't admit it.

Doyle recovered himself enough to say:

'It must've been done soon after they returned from Ashby. Jubal, do you think it's possible Doctor Hicks did this? I mean the way he was behaving an' all he seemed real upset. Could that've been an act?'

'Whoever Wilton is I'd say he must be a good actor. I must admit I don't see how a doctor could fake the skills he has. But who knows? Doctors are trusted instinctively and as Stroud pointed out to Miss Geddings not many people know what a doctor does. Let's hope I find something in Juniper Creek to clear this up.'

'Amen to that.'

Juniper Creek was the only place left. That morning Judd had received a reply to his telegram – the United States Marshals' Service had no knowledge of anyone called Rufus Wilton. And Marston was almost at the end of the judge's papers without having come across the name. That seemed strange to Judd but he thought that perhaps the episode with Wilton had been embedded so deeply in Geddings's mind he didn't need to write anything down.

'Simon, what's to do about the bodies? Where should they be buried?'

'At Saint Anne's.' Doyle didn't even have to think about that. 'The Proctors were regular churchgoers. Made the journey into town near every Sunday.'

'All right. We'll leave them be then. Send the undertaker out as soon as we get back.'

'Leave 'em like this?' Doyle waved his hand at the flies.

'We'll shut the room up as tight as possible.' Judd put a hand on the other man's shoulder for a moment. 'It won't make any difference to the Proctors.'

'Guess not.'

While Doyle started to shut the doors and windows, Judd went outside. He stood for a moment, taking deep breaths, glad to be out in the open. He felt . . . well, what did he feel? Angry? Anguished? All he knew was that he had to find out who Wilton was and stop him, before he could do anything more like this.

Wanting to do something to take his mind off what he'd seen, he unhitched the horse from the wagon and led it into the corral, making sure it and the other horses there had enough feed and water to last several days. The supplies in the wagon would have to stay where they were.

'Jubal.'

He looked up to see Doyle over by the barn. The man beckoned to him.

'See here, tracks of a horse. Fresh tracks.'

Judd bent to study them. The horse had been ridden in not from the road but from the direction of the nearby foothills. It had stood tied up for a while before being ridden out again the same way.

'It could belong to Wilton,' he agreed. 'Did you find anything in the house?'

'No.'

'Then we might as well follow the tracks. See where they lead.'

'If they continue through the hills they'll come into Ashby somewhere along by the river.'

'A route someone who didn't want to be seen might take?'

'Yeah. The quickest way too. Quicker than by the road.'

Judd was a good tracker. Anyway the tracks were easy to follow. If they belonged to Wilton he'd made no effort to hide them. The two men rode along in silence, alone with their thoughts.

Before long they entered the trees and started up the slope of the hillside. It was cool and quiet amongst the pines, undergrowth thick on either side. Judd was in the lead and suddenly his horse gave a frightened whinny, stopped and backed up, almost unseating Judd.

'Come on, girl.'

But the mare refused to go any further.

'Something's spooking her,' Doyle said. 'Wonder what? It's not Wilton, is it?' He sounded scared.

'Doubt it. If he's any sense he'll be back in Ashby.'

All the same Judd eased his guns in their holsters before dismounting. He handed the horse's reins to Doyle and went a little way into the undergrowth. A pile of leaves and branches lying beneath a tree had recently been disturbed, perhaps by some scavenging animal. On top of it were several bones. And when Judd looked closer he saw they formed a hand and part of an arm.

'Hell!' he exclaimed and stumbled backwards in surprise.

'What is it?'

'A skeleton.'

Doyle joined Judd, who began to brush away the leaves and a layer of earth. The skeleton had not been well buried and was soon revealed.

'It's a man,' Doyle stated. 'Or rather was.'

After scraping about in the rest of the earth under and around the tree, Judd said:

'Yeah and that's about all we can say for sure.' He stood up, wiping his hands free of dirt. 'There's nothing else left to say who he was or how long he's lain here.'

No clothes. Nothing personal.

'Any ideas?'

Doyle shook his head. 'None.'

'I think he was murdered before being buried here.'

'How do you know?'

'Look.' Judd pointed to the skull. 'The side of his head has been smashed in.'

'Could that've been an accident? Or mebbe done by an animal?'

'Perhaps. But I don't think so. Anyway, if it wasn't a murder why hide the body? OK, so it wasn't hidden all that well but how likely was it to be found?'

'Not likely at all,' Doyle admitted. 'No one comes up into these hills less'n they're searching for stray cattle. And then chances are they wouldn't find this grave. Hell, no one has up till now, have they? But what was he doing up here in the first place?'

Judd hazarded a guess.

'Perhaps his killer met him on the way into Ashby, decided to rob him and suggested this was a short cut into town or maybe said they'd have to camp out for the night as Ashby was too far away to make it before nightfall. The victim, a stranger to the area, knew no better and fell in with his killer's plans.'

Doyle nodded. 'It sounds as good a reason as any. So how do we find out who he was?'

'I don't see how we can,' Judd said with a little shrug. 'He could be anyone. Coming and going from anywhere. At any time. There's nothing to give us a starting point. His killer left not even a scrap of clothing. Simon,' he put a hand on the other man's shoulder and said, 'it probably hasn't got anything to do with Wilton. This body could have been here for years.'

Doyle didn't look convinced.

'Yeah, and he could've been here for a short while

and weather and animals turned him into a skeleton,' he said in a gloomy tone.

'I guess we'll never know. And there's too much else to worry about at the moment. So why don't we leave the bones here and get Pat to ride out with the undertaker? If he takes the bones down to the ranch they can be carried back to Ashby with the Proctors' bodies. Perhaps the reverend will be able to find a spot in the cemetery for them.'

'Yeah, good idea,' Doyle agreed. 'Christ, Jubal, what the hell else is going to happen? Ashby used to be a quiet good town and now look at it. I wish I'd never heard of that damn Wilton!'

It was late evening when Judd and Doyle neared the river. The sun was reddening the western sky and a breeze was picking up, riffling the water into tiny waves. Amongst the rocks and shale the trail disappeared.

Judd rode up and down the banks of the river in either direction. But he found no trace of any more tracks.

'It's almost as if it's done on purpose,' he said, as he returned to Doyle.

'How d'you mean?'

'Well, it's as if Wilton let us believe we were being skilful in following the trail whereas actually the bastard was letting us do so. And he's the skilful one because he knows how to hide it so well we'll never find it again.' Judd's whole body was tense with anger. He didn't like being ridiculed. And so far that was what Wilton had succeeded in doing.

Doyle pushed his hat to the back of his head and

wiped his forehead.

'And once he reaches the other side of the river the path there is too well travelled. We'll never pick his horse's tracks out amongst all the others. Dammit.'

Judd took a deep breath, swallowing his temper.

'Well, there's not any more we can do right now.'

'Guess not. Are you still leaving tomorrow?'

'Yeah, in the morning, real early. Get a good start before it turns too hot.'

'OK. I'll have Pat open up the livery for you. And, Jubal, be careful. You've been shot at once. Wilton could decide to try again.'

CHAPTER SIXTEEN

It was still dark, with dawn barely streaking the sky, when Judd walked through empty streets down to the livery. A yawning Pat Fisher was there before him, having opened up, and was getting the mare ready again. For this trip Judd would probably need her stamina.

'Good luck, Marshal,' he said as Judd mounted up.

'Thanks. I'll be as quick as I can.'

David Marston had worked out the best route for him to take. It led him down through the pine forest that surrounded the town. At the bottom of the slope the trees thinned out, the trail emerging into a long valley. On the far side was a stand of misshapen rock and more trees. By the time he crossed the valley, dawn had fully broken, lighting the country.

Several times Judd glanced along his back trail but no one and nothing moved behind him. He wasn't being followed. Rufus Wilton remained in Ashby.

'Oh, look, Barbara, here comes Mr Doyle.' Nora pointed towards the marshal who strode along the sidewalk, nodding to one or two passers-by.

'Good morning, Marshal,' Barbara said as they came face to face with the man.

Doyle raised his hat and blushed furiously.

'Miss Geddings, Mrs Wood,' he managed to say before coming to a stop.

Taking pity on him, Nora said:

'We've just visited the judge's grave so Barbara could lay fresh flowers by the cross.'

'Yes, and now we're on our way back to the hotel where I'm meeting Reverend Stroud. He's going to accompany me to the real estate office.'

'Oh, er, yeah.' Doyle's mind refused to think of anything more to say and he watched helplessly as the two women walked on.

'Really, he's impossible,' Barbara said once they were out of earshot. 'How he ever made marshal I'll never know.'

Nora smiled. 'He's shy and some of his shyness might be to do with you.'

'Me? I don't see why he should be shy of me.'

'Never mind, dear. And of course he's a worried man.'

'I'm not surprised,' Barbara said acidly. 'All these murders and he doesn't seem capable of doing anything to solve them.'

Nora was right. Doyle was worried. He had just come from Doctor Hicks who had more or less recovered from his shock at finding the Proctors. Unfortunately he hadn't seen anything to help catch their killer; in just the same way as there were no witnesses to the

113

killings of Old Roger or the judge. Pat Fisher hadn't found any bloodstained clothing and the town council was demanding results, especially after what had happened to one of its members.

He let himself into his office. It was quiet and cool inside. He was glad to have a few moments alone so he could think and put his thoughts in order.

Something was on his mind. Had been since yesterday. And now he realized what it was.

Out at the Proctors' ranch, he and Judd had wondered whether Hicks could be Rufus Wilton. But now Doyle knew that if Wilton had ridden the horse whose trail they followed he couldn't be. Hicks didn't ride. He went everywhere in his buggy. Had been driving his buggy yesterday. And if Wilton hadn't ridden the horse then who had been out at the ranch and why did the trail suddenly disappear?

The only reason they had suspected Hicks was because of what Reverend Stroud had told Miss Geddings. Why had he done so? Was it because the two men disliked one another and each took every opportunity to criticize the other? Or was it so that Stroud looked important in front of Miss Geddings?

Or was it . . . oh God! It couldn't be, could it? Surely it was just as impossible for a reverend as for a doctor to be a cold-blooded murderer?

But supposing it was possible?

Doyle stood up and took several turns round his office. Supposing Stroud was Rufus Wilton? It had to be easier to pretend to be a preacher than a doctor and no one ever queried where Stroud was because he could be anywhere: in the church, out visiting his

114

parishioners in the town or in the country, or, well, anywhere!

And Miss Barbara Geddings was becoming friendly with him, spending time in his company.

God! What should he do? What the hell could he do?

He had no proof. And as he couldn't talk to Miss Geddings without blushing bright red and stumbling over every word he had no way to convince her that it might be true. She would never believe him. Would laugh at him. Might tell Stroud and so, if he was Wilton, warn him.

Maybe he would talk to Stroud, ask him why he thought Hicks was the killer. That was something he, as marshal, would be expected to do and wouldn't alert the man to anything wrong. He could also keep a watch on Miss Geddings, make sure she was safe. Otherwise best keep his suspicions to himself until Judd got back. With luck he wouldn't be long.

Judd rode hard and steadily for a very long day and that night camped out on the edge of the desert. The country was empty, except for a few spiny-backed lizards. Once a rattlesnake almost spooked his horse, before slithering away. There were plenty of different kinds of cactus. It was hot, the sun shining mercilessly out of a molten blue sky. Airless.

He reached Juniper Creek in the afternoon of the second day. A line of sycamore trees indicated the course of the almost dry creek, very little water flowing over its white stony bed. He came to a narrow bridge and then he was in the town. Dusty streets.

Three or four stores. A café and a small boarding-house. Several saloons. Horses and wagons tied to railings. A few people wandering about – ranchers and cowboys. A couple of miners. No women. That was about it.

Judd left the mare at the livery stable and asked for directions to the courthouse. Juniper Creek didn't have one. It did have a new jailhouse and that included a room out back where trials were held.

The jailhouse was situated beyond a plaza with a fountain playing in the middle, round which a number of Mexicans lazed in the sun. As with all the other buildings the jailhouse was made of adobe with small windows and inside it struck as cool; a welcome relief.

'Hi, help you?' A young man, growing a wispy beard in an obvious attempt to make him appear older, looked up from the one desk. He wore a marshal's star.

'Yeah. I'm Jubal Judd—'

'Oh, yeah, Marshal, we've been expecting you. David Marston from up in Ashby telegraphed you were on your way. Clay Macintosh.' He stood up and shook Judd's hand enthusiastically. 'Ain't often we get a United States marshal calling on us in Juniper Creek. I understand you want to look at anything we've got on an old case 'bout Rufus Wilton.'

'Yeah.'

Macintosh's face creased into a frown.

'I got all the papers out but I'm afraid there ain't much. Back then no one bothered about keeping detailed records. Just Mr So-and-So charged with

116

whatever and either found guilty or innocent. Along
with the sentence.'

'You know Judge Geddings has been murdered,
don't you?'

The frown deepened. 'Yeah, we did hear and then
Mr Marston also let us know. A real shame. The judge
was a real good man. A real hard worker. It wasn't
easy for him to get here, we only have a stage calling
twice a week, but he always came as quick as he could
whenever we had anyone held for trial.'

'When was he here last?'

'Three months ago. You don't think that had
anything to do with his murder, do you?' Macintosh
suddenly sounded worried.

'No. His murderer was living in Ashby. Can I see
what you have got?'

'Course. I've put everything out in the back room.
You're welcome to go through it. And I'll get you a
coffee. But there ain't much.' Macintosh repeated
his warning.

And Judd quickly realized the marshal was right.

The file consisted of just two or three pages, most
of it written out in Judge Geddings's crabbed hand-
writing. It told him very little. Nothing about Wilton
himself; neither his age nor appearance. Just that he
was charged with robbery, the murder of two people
and shooting at the marshal when trapped. That he
was found guilty and sentenced to be hanged but
before sentence could be carried out he had escaped
and disappeared into the desert.

Discouraged he went back to the marshal's office
where Macintosh was pretending to be busy.

'I suppose you don't remember anything about Wilton's trial?'

Macintosh shook his head.

' 'Fore my time. But there is someone who might help you.'

'Oh?'

'Yeah. The marshal who arrested Wilton, Ben Hattersley, he still lives around here. He remembers what happened right enough. It's 'bout all he ever talks of.'

CHAPTER SEVENTEEN

'Yeah, I remember Rufus Wilton only too damn well,' Ben Hattersley said. 'He was the reason I quit being a lawman.'

It hadn't taken Judd long to reach the ranch Hattersley owned, for it was situated just outside of town, at the head of the creek. He lived with his wife, Louisa, and Judd learned they had several children, all of whom were working out on the range. It didn't seem all that prosperous a place but perhaps that was due more to the country than the Hattersleys.

The house wasn't much more than a three-room shack, with little in the way of furniture. The outbuildings had a ramshackle air. But both Hattersley and his wife greeted Judd affably enough and invited him in to share the evening meal of beef-stew and plum pie, while Hattersley agreed he was willing to talk about Wilton.

Hattersley was fifty. A tall man but running to fat with a stomach overhanging his trousers. He had sparse brown hair and wrinkles at the corners of his blue eyes. Louisa, who was a few years younger, was also plump. Which made Judd hope his portion of stew might be both substantial and well cooked. While Louisa took herself off to prepare the meal, the two men sat in sagging chairs on the sagging porch.

Hattersley poured out glasses of home-made lemonade and stared off towards the distant smudge of hills.

'What happened?' Judd prompted.

'I remember when Wilton arrived in Juniper Creek. It was spring, before it got too hot. Eighteen sixty-three. He was fifteen and looked like many another scrawny kid down on his luck. I caught him stealing eggs from someone's henhouse. He told me he was an orphan. Said his parents were killed early in the Civil War by Jayhawkers so he'd fled the farm and headed west.' Hattersley drank some of his lemonade and turned to look at Judd. 'At the time neither I nor anyone else doubted the kid. We'd heard dreadful stories of the war back East and we all felt sorry for him. Later,' he shrugged, 'I had my doubts.'

'You think he killed his own parents?'

Hattersley shrugged again.

'He certainly never made no secret of the fact that he'd been unhappy at home. Had plenty of tales of a drunken father who beat him regular. Mebbe he was telling the truth 'bout that. Something musta made him turn out like he did. That kid was outta my league.'

Out of most people's, Judd thought.

'Later I did try to find out what had happened to his folks but communications were messed up after the Civil War and there was no one either willing or able to send me any information.'

'It's obvious he's clever at changing both his name and his personality so perhaps Rufus Wilton wasn't his real name. Perhaps his whole story was a lie.'

Hattersley nodded in agreement and then went on with his story of what had happened in Juniper Creek.

'Like I said, most people here felt sorry for him. The town was a deal smaller in them days than now. Everyone knew everyone. It was a harsh environment and a tough way of life. So people did their best to help one another.'

'And so someone helped Wilton?'

Hattersley nodded again.

'A couple called Adam and Maud Roberts got to hear 'bout the boy. They owned a small trading post, not far from this ranch actually. Sometimes the townspeople went there but mostly it served the Apache Indians, who, in those days, lived in the hills. They never caused no trouble. Helped by the fact that the Roberts never cheated 'em. 'Sides the store, the Roberts had a vegetable-patch, ran a few cattle. They decided they needed help so they took the kid in.'

Hattersley drained his lemonade and paused to pour himself out more. He held out the bottle to Judd and, it still being hot and airless, Judd passed over his glass for a refill.

'Now, Marshal, I ain't saying they were an ideal couple to look after a boy of fifteen. They were a stern, God-fearing pair. In fact Roberts did a bit of preaching, of the hell-fire kind, in his spare time. I ain't got any way of knowing but I wouldn't bet against Roberts deciding a beating or two was the best way to drive the devil out of a boy.'

'Even though that devil could just be normal high spirits?'

'Which at the time everyone else thought was the case. Because while the kid got drunk on occasion and liked to fight the other boys he didn't do anything *bad*.' Hattersley sighed. 'Although I suppose actually the Roberts' were right and the rest of us was wrong.'

'And I guess it would've been hard work and a lonely life?' Judd glanced out at the valley that stretched endlessly before him.

'That it was. Adam and Maud only got into town 'bout once a month and there wasn't much happening in town when they got there! So I guess what I'm saying is that the kid didn't have a great life out at the store but at the same time they did take him in when he was down on his luck. They fed and clothed him and did the best by him as they saw fit.'

'It obviously didn't suit Wilton,' Judd said. 'But then perhaps whatever anyone did wouldn't have suited him. Perhaps he was just that sort who liked to cause trouble.'

'Mebbe.'

'I read he was charged with murder. I take it that was the two Roberts?'

'Yeah. That was how he thanked 'em.' A note of anger entered Hattersley's voice. 'Wilton began robbing both them and their customers. Small amounts. Trinkets. That kind of thing. Every damn chance he got. Dunno why. He couldn't have hoped to steal enough to run away.'

'Perhaps it was just something to do.' Judd frowned. Wilton had started to do the same kind of thing in Ashby.

'He didn't bother to hide what he was doing so, of course, it weren't long before Adam realized he was stealing from 'em. He must've confronted him. And so Wilton killed them both.' Hattersley paused and even after all this time his face paled under its leathery suntan. 'Let me tell you, Mr Judd, I'd seen some bad sights before. Even some bodies tortured and left by Indians. I ain't never seen anything like what that kid did to them folks.'

Just like the Proctors, Judd thought. He didn't ask Hattersley for details because it was obvious the man didn't want to remember what he'd seen and had had to bury.

'And I think there might've been others he killed.'

'Oh, who?'

'Supposing a lone, old Indian called at the store; well, if he didn't get back to his camp who would his relatives complain to? What about other lonely travellers who wouldn't have no one to miss 'em? I didn't have no way of proving it, then or now, but there were rumours 'bout some who came to Juniper Creek and then weren't seen again. And once he was caught the kid no longer felt the need to put on an act but sure had a look of liking it. And the Roberts' were killed so well, if you know what I mean, they couldn't, just couldn't've been his first victims.'

'At least you caught him.' Judd thought that might give the old lawman a degree of comfort.

Instead Hattersley sounded scornful.

'Oh yeah. All too easily.'

'You think he wanted to be caught?'

'I think the bastard let himself be caught, yeah. Wanted to let folks know exactly what he'd done. Wanted his moment of glory in standing trial. He went on the run but he left a clear trail behind him and he holed up at an empty shack that was easy to surround. Then he gave himself up, almost without a fight, just fired at me once or twice, the bullets not coming anywhere near. And so I took him back to Juniper Creek. At the time I didn't think nothing of it being only too pleased to catch the bastard but afterwards . . .' Hattersley shook his head and, sounding angry at both Wilton and himself, went on: 'I had the feeling Wilton had deliberately fooled me like he fooled most folks.'

'What did he say?' Judd asked. 'When you brought him back to town?'

'Oh, that he hadn't done it. But all the time he had this smirk on his face what said he'd done it all right and that he was pleased with himself. Right cocky little bastard! I contacted Judge Geddings and he arrived a few days later. Wilton had his moment in court right enough and he shot his way out of it too.'

'Out of the court itself?' Judd was surprised. The papers he'd read hadn't mentioned that, only that

Wilton had escaped; and he thought that meant from the jailhouse afterwards.

'Yeah. Grabbed my deputy's gun and wounded him so bad he later died. Killed his lawyer. Shot a couple of others. And vanished into the desert. And this time he left no trail behind him. And so, Mr Judd, that was what he wanted most of all. To show how clever he was. That not only could he deceive everyone but he could escape from justice any time he wanted to.'

'He did something similar in Ashby,' said Judd, remembering the trail that was easy to follow until it disappeared at the river.

'Left me and the posse no choice but to return to town. I sent out messages to other lawmen around here but we never heard another thing 'bout the bastard. And soon after I gave up being marshal. After seeing the evil in that kid's heart and mind I didn't feel up to the job no more.'

'What did you think happened to him?'

'I wanted to believe he died in the desert but in my heart I didn't. He was the type of bastard to survive. Whenever I read in the newspapers of some bad killings that no one had been arrested for I wondered if he was responsible.' Hattersley sighed. 'Then when I heard 'bout Judge Geddings being shot I reckoned, I knew, that after all these years the little sonofabitch had caught up with the judge and killed him. Like he meant to do back in that court-room. At least I stopped him doing that.'

'So, if he was fifteen when he arrived in Juniper Creek how old was he when all this happened?'

'Nineteen.'

'That'd make him thirty-three now.'

'Yeah.'

'What did he look like?'

'He had dark-brown hair. Brown eyes. Scrawny. Quite tall. Thin lips.'

Judd sat up straight, his heart beginning to beat fast.

'Hattersley, would you come back to Ashby with me? See if you can recognize Wilton?'

A look almost of panic came into the man's eyes. He stood up, went over to the railing, leant his hands on it. It creaked ominously beneath his weight.

'I dunno 'bout that, Marshal. It's a helluva way. I'm real busy here at the moment. Anyway I doubt I'd recognize Wilton after all this time.'

Even though Judge Geddings had. Judd sighed, wondering if he ought to force the man to go with him. There seemed little point. It was obvious that even after fourteen years Hattersley was still scarred and scared by his encounter with Wilton.

'That's a damn pity,' he said, 'but I can't make you go.'

CHAPTER EIGHTEEN

Louisa Hattersley refused to let her husband and
Judd talk about the old case, or any other matters of
the law, during the evening meal. So talk mostly
concerned the difficulties of ranching in the desert,
the extremes of weather and life in Juniper Creek.
And the Hattersley children, of whom Ben and
Louisa were very proud.

Judd had booked a room in the boarding-house,
meaning to return to Ashby early the following
morning. He left the ranch with the sun going down
in an orange ball of flame.

Afterwards, as the air cooled towards night,
Hattersley went out on the porch to enjoy a glass of
whiskey. Having finished the washing-up, Louisa
joined him. She linked her arm through his and
stared out at the shadows enveloping the desert.

'You think I should've gone with him, don't you?'
Hattersley broke the silence.

Louisa sighed. She knew how Rufus Wilton – the
kind of person he was and the fact that Hattersley
had not succeeded in bringing him to justice – still

haunted her husband's dreams. Knew he didn't want to be involved but wanted to forget. Yet all the time Wilton was still out there, free to continue robbing and murdering, she also knew Ben would never be able to forget him.

'Maybe,' she said. 'It might have helped both you and Mr Judd.'

'I told him all I could. Anyway I think the marshal has a good idea of who Wilton is.'

'I hope so. Oh, Ben, I'm not criticizing you.' Louisa squeezed his arm. 'You've always done what was right. Done your best. No one could have asked for a better lawman and I couldn't ask for a better husband.' She was sure he would do what was right now, however much he didn't want to.

And after a few moments Hattersley said:

'OK, I'll go with Mr Judd.'

Louisa smiled. 'I'm sure he'll be grateful for your help.'

The boarding-house room was grubby. And the bed was not only lumpy, with a lumpy pillow, Judd suspected the mattress contained bugs. It was too hot and stuffy, even with the window wide open, to sleep. And he had too much on his mind as well.

He pulled a chair up by the window and sat there, thinking.

He felt disturbed by all Hattersley had told him. How could a young man of nineteen, still a boy really, kill so readily and so nastily? What had happened to turn Wilton into a killer? Was it his harsh childhood, as Hattersley suspected, or did he have some evil inside him that he would have become what he had whatever sort of upbringing he enjoyed? After all many another boy experienced beatings without turning wild. Judd could remember a few beatings of his own.

He hoped that none of that mattered any more. For now, thanks to the lawman's description of Wilton as a young man, Judd was sure he knew the identity of Rufus Wilton. There was only one person it could be. Even though he'd tried to hide his lips with a beard it was obvious to anyone who looked at him how thin they were.

As soon as dawn broke he'd be on his way back. He wondered whether or not to send a message over the telegraph to Doyle. He decided not to as he didn't want to risk Wilton finding out and making his escape before Judd got there to arrest him.

But he wished it wasn't so far. . . .

Wished he knew what was happening in Ashby. . . .

Doyle was annoyed. He had not yet found the time to speak to Reverend Stroud.

For a start Stroud was out with Miss Geddings, helping her to inspect the few houses the real estate office had for sale. The following day some stupid cowboys decided to go on the rampage down in the red-light district and he and Fisher were busy rounding them up and jailing the ringleaders. And dealing with the paperwork. Then Doyle had had to attend a lengthy meeting of the town council after which all he'd wanted to do was go home.

And lastly, today the reverend was occupied with

the funeral service for the Proctors. Doyle didn't like to bother him while he was preparing for that.

By now anyway Doyle had doubts about the reverend's guilt. He appeared so sincere and everyone (except Doctor Hicks) liked him; he had to be genuine. Perhaps he would leave confronting him until Judd got back rather than make a fool of himself. This was the third day the marshal had been away. He should, with luck, be here the next day.

He was waiting for Fisher to return from whatever it was he was doing so he could go home when Nora Wood came in. She looked harassed and worried.

'What's the matter?' he asked, pulling out a chair for her. Now what, he was thinking, but whatever he thought might have happened the reality was worse.

'It's Barbara. She seems to be missing.' Nora spoke breathlessly, her hands clenched together in her lap.

'Missing? What do you mean?' Doyle's heart skipped several beats.

'Just that. She went out this afternoon, soon after the Proctors' funeral, saying she would be back about five o'clock in time to get ready for dinner. It's now gone six. And there's no sign of her.'

'Where was Miss Geddings going?'

'To change the flowers on her father's grave and then do a little bit of shopping.'

'Have you been to the church?'

'No.' Nora shook her head. 'I thought it best to come straight here, although I did look in on one or two of the stores on my way. She wasn't in any of them and the few people I spoke to said they hadn't seen her. Oh dear, Marshal, perhaps I'm worrying unnecessarily, but it's so unlike her. When Barbara says she's going to do something she does it, especially when she knows how I feel.'

Doyle touched the woman on the shoulder.

'Don't worry. I'll go and look for her. You go back to the hotel. She might even be there by now.'

Although he'd told Nora not to worry, Doyle found himself worrying. Very much. He too asked about Barbara in the stores and then went to the cemetery. When he entered the gates there was no sign of the girl. He walked up to the judge's grave. Fresh flowers were placed by it, so she had been here. But she wasn't now. So where had she gone? Let her be all right, he thought, please don't let anything have happened to her. Don't let Wilton have hurt her. He couldn't come up with any reason why Wilton would do so, except that she was Judge Geddings's daughter.

He was debating what to do when he heard someone call his name. Turning he saw Reverend Stroud walking towards him from the direction of his house.

'Is something wrong, Marshal?'

'Did you see Miss Geddings after the funeral?'

'Why, yes, she was here, oh, about three o'clock I suppose. She comes every day to visit her father's grave. A most devoted daughter. I spoke to her for a while before I went back home to write my sermon for this Sunday.'

'Do you know what time she left?'

'No, I don't. As I say when I left her she was still here by the grave. What's the matter?'

'She hasn't returned to the hotel and Mrs Wood

was anxious about where she had gone.'

'Oh my.' Stroud's hands twisted together. 'Where can she be? I wish I could help. I hope she's all right. With all that's going on . . . I can't believe how bad things have become.' He glanced up at where the four graves of the Proctor family lay side by side. 'Who else is going to be killed? When will Marshal Judd be back?'

'Tomorrow I hope. Reverend, while I'm here I want to talk to you about how you told Miss Geddings that you suspected Doctor Hicks of being the killer.' Doyle decided he might as well take the opportunity to question Stroud. However anxious he was about Barbara, the few moments he spent doing so would make no difference to whatever had happened to her.

'Oh goodness me.' Stroud looked startled. 'Oh, lord, I wish I'd never said anything.'

'But you did do so.'

'Yes I know. Oh dear. I don't know . . . it just seemed . . . I have no evidence. Umm, look, Mr Doyle, it's hot out here and we might be seen, so why don't we go into the church? We can talk there without being disturbed and it'll be cool. And maybe Miss Geddings will be there too, praying. In fact, come to think of it she did mention she might do so. Perhaps that's the answer.' Stroud smiled.

'Yeah, OK.' And hoping the reverend was right Doyle followed him down the slope to Saint Anne's.

Pat Fisher sat at his desk, wondering what to do. He hadn't been a deputy for long and right then he

THE LONG DARK TRAIL

wished he wasn't one now. He wanted to go home but he didn't like to leave the place empty, what with the prisoners in the cells – Doyle was fussy about things like that – and the fact that now both Miss Geddings and Marshal Doyle had disappeared!

He looked at his watch for the tenth time in ten minutes. Time was crawling by, yet at the same time hurrying by so that it was well into the evening. Was getting dark. Where were they? What was happening? What should he do? Sit tight. Start a search. He felt quite unable to deal with the situation by himself.

He decided to go to the hotel and find out if Miss Geddings had returned there. If not he'd seek help from Doctor Hicks and Bruce Anderson. They were members of the town council. They earned much more than he did, were more important too, and would know what to do.

CHAPTER NINETEEN

'Marshal Doyle. Mr Doyle, please wake up.'

The voice reached him from what seemed a long way away. Doyle blinked open his eyes. Wherever he was it was very dark, the only light coming from a couple of cracks in the wooden ceiling. It was also hot and the air stale, making it difficult to breathe.

He found himself lying on a hard mattress. His head hurt and, with a little groan, he closed his eyes again, wanting to go back to sleep.

'Mr Doyle, wake up.' The voice, a girl's, was both urgent and very scared.

Making a reluctant effort, Doyle looked round, more carefully this time. And lifted his head slightly, ignoring the throbbing pain. By the little light he saw Barbara Geddings sitting on a hard-backed chair near to him. And he saw also she was tied to it, with her arms bound behind her and ropes round her waist and ankles.

'My God!' he exclaimed and tried to sit up.

Big mistake. Not only did his head spin wildly he also realized his hands were secured to a ring in the wall with his own handcuffs! His arms ached from the awkward position they were held in and he couldn't move very far.

'What the hell is going on?' he demanded.

'We're Rufus Wilton's prisoners,' Barbara said quietly.

'What! How can we be?' Doyle sank down on the mattress. But of course they could be; they were. And with a sinking of his heart he realized he'd been right: Reverend Stroud was Rufus Wilton. 'Where are we? Do you know?'

Barbara nodded.

'We're in some sort of basement beneath the church. Stroud was quite boastful about how he'd built it by himself—'

'Yeah, I remember when he first arrived he did a lot of work on the church.'

'From what he said I don't think anyone else even knows it exists. And even if they do why should they look for us here? When they all trust and love their preacher!' Barbara's voice rose in fright.

'Are you all right?' Doyle was very concerned about the girl. 'He hasn't hurt you, has he?'

'Apart from forcibly dragging me down here and trussing me up, no.'

Thank God for that.

'But I've no doubt he intends to hurt me, and you, in the not too distant future.'

Doyle didn't doubt that either.

'What happened?'

'Oh, I was fooled by him in the same way as nearly everyone else.' Barbara gave a bitter laugh. 'I should have listened to Nora. But, no . . . So when he came up to me as I was leaving father's grave and said he had something to show me in the church I didn't hesitate in going with him.'

'You couldn't have known. I did exactly the same.'

Doyle could remember going through the door into the church's dim interior. And that was all. He didn't know who he was most furious with: Wilton, for outwitting him, or himself for being so easily outwitted. He hadn't believed he was in any danger but that if he was he could handle it. He should have been more careful and he hadn't been. He deserved whatever Wilton had in mind for him but Barbara didn't.

'So Stroud boasted when he carried you down here. He thinks he's so damned clever!' Barbara paused. 'Anyway, once he'd made sure he and I were alone in the church he suddenly admitted being Rufus Wilton. For a moment I thought he was joking. When I realized he wasn't, it was too late. He grabbed me and tied me up. Why now, do you think?'

'Probably because he knows he risks being found out if he stays in Ashby much longer. He can't afford to wait until Judd gets back from Juniper Creek in case Judd has found evidence of his guilt. He's getting ready to run again.'

'And he wants to kill us before he goes?'

Doyle didn't answer. It wasn't really a question because Barbara knew only too well what Wilton was like and what was in his mind.

'How long have we been here, do you know?'

Barbara shook her head.

'It seems like years. Oh, Simon, what are we going to do?'

Despite their predicament Doyle's heart soared. She had called him by his Christian name!

'Escape,' he said bluntly.

'But how?'

'Hush.'

Doyle's ears had caught the sound of a scraping noise. Almost at the same time a trapdoor in the middle of the ceiling was lifted up and Reverend Stroud appeared in the opening. He jumped down. He held a candle, which he placed on a wooden box. By its light, Doyle saw that the man had an entirely different look about him. He wore the same clothes, had done nothing to his appearance but his face held a triumphant smirk so it was no longer surprising that, even after fourteen years, Judge Geddings had recognized him: he was truly Rufus Wilton.

'So you're awake! At last.' Stroud/Wilton came to a halt by Doyle and kicked him hard, making him grunt in pain.

He giggled and Doyle, feeling at a considerable disadvantage, managed to sit up. He couldn't stop Wilton doing whatever he wanted but at least he wasn't going to take it without a certain amount of defiance.

'Well, Marshal, how d'you like my hidy-hole? No one would ever suspect it was here. In the same way no one would ever suspect me.'

'Judge Geddings did.'

'Oh, him! Stupid bastard. Forgive me, dear Miss Geddings. Shoulda shot him back in Juniper Creek.

Telling me how I'd done wrong and I oughta repent my sins before they stretched my neck. The nerve of it when old Roberts and his sour wife deserved to die. Woulda shot him too but that damn marshal got in the way. Still I got him in the end.'

It was hard to decide whether Wilton was angry, excited or simply pleased with himself. He seemed quite calm, at odds with his words.

Barbara gave a little cry of horror and despair.

'Don't fret, little darling.' Wilton stroked the girl's face, laughing as she tried to pull away from him.

'Leave her be,' Doyle said angrily.

'Or what? What you gonna do 'bout it? Think you're so damn clever don't you? Just because you're a lawman. Well, you ain't clever at all.'

'Nor are you. You'll be caught sooner or later.'

'Oh yeah? Ain't been up till now!'

Doyle could see the man's eyes were glittering with, what, madness perhaps? He feared what Wilton might do, and he could see that Barbara was getting very frightened, but then Wilton seemed to gain control of himself.

Wilton picked up the candle to shine it round the basement.

'You never said what you thought of it down here,' he said. 'Makes a perfect hiding-place, don't it?'

It was as if the man really expected praise for building it and Doyle didn't bother to answer but said instead:

'What exactly are you doing in Ashby? What made you become its preacher?'

'You ain't worked that out either, have you?'

138

'No.' Doyle sighed, getting mighty fed up with the man's boasting. 'But then I'm obviously not as intelligent as you.'

Wilton appeared pleased by that, believing Doyle meant it, nodding in agreement.

'That skeleton you and that stupid US marshal found? That was the real Reverend Oliver Stroud. Met up with him on the road. Silly bastard done told me how he was coming from California to take up a position as preacher here. How Ashby was a wealthy town and likely to get wealthier. Seemed like too good an opportunity to miss.'

'So you killed him?'

'Sure did. Bashed his head in when he weren't looking.' Another little cry from Barbara made Wilton laugh even more. 'Stole his clothes and his Bible and buried his body. Then I came on here.'

'But you aren't a preacher,' Barbara objected. 'What made you think you could get away with pretending to be one?'

'Hell, Miss Geddings, people believe what they want to. I've been lots of things in the past and no one has ever questioned or doubted me.' Wilton thrust his face forward. 'I've always been able to fool people. It's oh so simple. All you gotta do is act the way they think you should. But now, thanks to your goddamn father, dear Miss Geddings, and the interference of Mr goddamn Judd, it's time to move on. Pity, I was enjoying myself here. And there were several more people I wanted to kill before I left.'

'Who?' Doyle asked.

'That stupid Doctor Hicks for one. Do you know I

think he's started to suspect me.'

'He's not so stupid, then.'

Wilton ignored that. 'D'you know, I just might wait for Mr Jubal Judd's return and kill him too. He should be back real soon. Silly of me perhaps but I think I'm prepared to take the chance because I ain't never killed a US marshal. Might be fun.'

'He'll know who you are,' Doyle said. 'He'll be on his guard.'

'Won't do him no good iffen I lay in wait for him.'

'You missed him before.'

'Shut up.' Wilton kicked Doyle again, obviously not liking to be reminded of his failures. 'Now.' He put his hands on his hips and leant back, surveying them both. 'What should I do with you two?'

'Get on with it,' Doyle snarled. 'You've obviously already made up your mind.'

Wilton grinned. 'Well, yeah, I have. See, I thought of all kinds of ways to kill you but then I decided how much better, how much funnier, just to leave you down here. Everyone'll be rushing about Ashby looking for you and here you'll be tied up and help-less beneath their feet! Unable to attract their atten-tion.'

'You bastard,' Doyle said, which made Wilton even happier.

'I ain't sure which'll happen first. Whether you'll starve to death before you run out of air, or iffen it'll be the other way round. Don't matter much. Either way you'll both be dead having watched each other suffer an agonizing death.' Laughing heartily, he rubbed his hands together. 'Couldn't be better. My only regret is I won't be around to see it. But I'll be able to imagine it.'

'You can't leave Miss Geddings down here. She hasn't done anything to hurt you.'

'Stop with the sermonizing,' Wilton shouted, starting to bounce up and down. 'Having been a preacher for the last few months I've had quite enough of goddamn sermons. And prayers. And hymns. And all the goddamn stupid people singing 'em. Oh and this here beard. That's coming off soon as I'm away from this stupid town.'

And without another word he took himself and his candle over to the trapdoor and climbed up through it. He shut it with a bang leaving Doyle and Barbara in darkness.

CHAPTER TWENTY

'He's mad, isn't he,' Barbara said.

'It's the only explanation I can come up with,' Doyle admitted.

'He's not still up there, is he? Watching us?'

Doyle looked up at the ceiling. Were any of the cracks large enough for Wilton to peer through? Was he above them in the church listening to what they said and mocking them? He didn't think Wilton would take the chance of someone seeing him and wondering what he was doing.

'No, don't worry, Barbara.' Doyle felt very brave calling her that but she didn't seem to mind. 'Barbara, I can feel the key to the handcuffs in my vest pocket.'

Wilton hadn't thought to search him. Nor had he gagged them. Perhaps he wasn't quite as clever as he thought he was. 'If I can get hold of it I'll be able to free myself. But I'll need your help.'

'All right.'

'Can you manoeuvre your way over to me?'

'I'll try.'

Barbara started to rock sideways, lifting the legs on one side of the chair slightly and then banging down again; making painfully slow progress. It was painful for herself too as her body was badly jolted with each movement.

At last she got to the mattress on which Doyle was sitting.

'Now what? I can't reach you from here so far above you.'

'You'll have to tip yourself over on top of me.'

Barbara grimaced but made no objection. She rocked the chair until it started to fall. Momentum took her the rest of the way. She landed on Doyle, knocking the breath out of both of them, the back of the chair hitting him in the face.

'The key is in my left-hand pocket.'

Straining against the ropes Wilton had tied so tightly, making her wrists bleed, Barbara's fingers scrabbled across Doyle's chest. They found the pocket and reached inside. With thumb and forefinger she managed to catch hold of the key.

'You'll have to get up and pass it to me.'

'Easier said than done,' Barbara muttered. Although she tried she was unable to gain any purchase.

'Roll over. You'll be able to get to your knees then. Go on, Barbara, you can do it. You don't want Wilton to win, do you?'

Gritting her teeth the girl slipped off Doyle and turned round, still on her knees, her back to him. He managed to lean down far enough for one of his hands to reach hers. He took the key from her and praying he wouldn't drop it, reached up and fumbled to put the key into the lock. After several attempts he undid the handcuffs. He was free!

After he'd rubbed feeling back into his arms and hands it was a matter of minutes to untie Barbara. She sat for a while, crying as she tried to move her arms and legs.

'Come on,' he urged. 'Get up. Walk up and down.' He helped the girl to stand and she clung to him. In his relief Doyle forgot about being nervous in her company and hugged her tightly.

'Up till now I hadn't realized how frightened I was,' she said with a little sob in her voice.

'We'll be all right now.' Doyle spoke with more confidence than he felt.

Wilton had taken his gun; he had no way to defend himself and Barbara if the man decided to come down here again. Well, time to face that when and if it happened. First they had to get out of the basement.

He went over to the trapdoor. He didn't expect it would open and, of course, it didn't. It was bolted from above. He picked up the chair and stood on it, shoving hard. It was no use. It wouldn't move. They were securely locked in.

'What are we going to do?' Barbara asked.

Doyle admitted defeat.

'There's nothing we can do except hope someone comes into the church looking for us and we can attract their attention. Someone will.' Sooner or later. 'And despite Wilton's boasting I'm sure we'll be able to hear if someone does and, more important, they'll be able to hear us. And I just bet Mr Judd will've found out enough to know Stroud is the one we're after.' He put an arm round the girl. 'Don't worry, we'll get out of here. Wilton won't get away with what he's done.'

'Meanwhile we wait?'

'I'm afraid so. Why don't we make ourselves as comfortable as we can?'

'On the floor?'

'You lie on the mattress and I'll lie on the floor.'

'No, Simon, share the mattress with me. Hold me close. That way I won't be so frightened.'

Doctor Hicks and Bruce Anderson had decided that a search should be made for Barbara and Marshal Doyle. Much to the annoyance of Nora, who was becoming more and more anxious with each passing moment, they also decided it was too late to do anything that night but the search would be started as soon as it was light the next day.

It revealed no trace of either Doyle or Barbara.

'But they must be somewhere,' Nora wailed. 'They can't both have disappeared into thin air!'

Nervously Pat Fisher ran a hand through his hair.

'But where are they? We've looked all over. No one's seen them. There's no sign of them. Anywhere.' He paused. 'You don't think Rufus Wilton has got them, do you?' He sounded very worried and scared.

'It's the only possible explanation.' Nora was even more worried. 'They wouldn't have gone off together without a word to someone. Besides, Barbara disappeared before Marshal Doyle. And he went to look for her.'

'Oh lord.' Fisher hoped fervently that Judd would soon return. If nothing happened to delay him he should be back some time that day.

'Well, Deputy, are you going to just sit there and do nothing?'

'Er, no, er, I'll look some more.' Anything to escape the woman's frightened glare. 'Perhaps I'll go to the church, ask Reverend Stroud if he's seen them. I never got to speak to him when I called there earlier this morning as he was out somewhere but he should be back now.'

'And I'll visit Doctor Hicks. Find out if he has any fresh ideas about where they could be. It's not even as if this is a big town.'

It was very hot, one of the hottest days of the year so far. Fisher was glad when he reached Saint Anne's and, spotting no one in the cemetery, felt he could look for the reverend in the cool of the church. He pushed open the door and went inside. To his disappointment he saw it was still empty. But maybe the preacher was in one of the rooms leading off the nave.

The deputy walked up the aisle and stopped at the door at one side of the altar. It had been locked earlier on but now it was open. Stroud must be around somewhere. Fisher went through into the vestry.

'Reverend,' he called.

Silence.

'You here?'

*

'What was that?' Doyle struggled to his feet.

'What?' Barbara was beside him, clutching at his coat-sleeve.

'I heard something.'

'Wilton?'

'No. There, listen, it's Pat! Pat, we're here!' Doyle called out as loudly as he could. His voice caught in his dry throat and he coughed.

'Don't let him go,' Barbara said in a panic-stricken voice.

Doyle swallowed several times and tried again.

'Here, Pat, we're here!'

'Marshal?' Fisher sounded very puzzled. But he'd heard them. 'Where are you?'

'Bang on the trapdoor,' Barbara said. 'Here, use my shoe.' She handed one of her shoes to Doyle.

Above them Fisher heard the knocking sound and glanced down. He quickly pulled away the rug lying in the middle of the room. It revealed the bolted trapdoor. He bent to undo it. As he did so he sensed a flicker of movement behind him. He half—turned round and a gun fired.

'That was a shot!' Barbara cried. 'What's happening?'

'Pat! Pat? You OK?' Doyle was frantic. Surely with rescue so near at hand their rescuer couldn't have been killed!

Hit in the arm, Fisher fell to the floor. As he landed he saw Reverend Stroud looming in the doorway. Not quite understanding what was going on, he still acted quickly. He slid back the bolt on the trap-door before slipping away behind a cupboard. Awkwardly he drew his gun with his left hand and fired several times, exchanging shots with Wilton.

Below, Doyle pushed the trapdoor open.

'Stay here,' he ordered Barbara and pulled himself through it. He dived for shelter.

'It's Stroud,' Fisher yelled. 'He's gone back into the church.'

'Give me your gun.' Doyle went to the door and peered round it. There was a shot. The bullet almost struck him. He returned the fire, without hoping to hit anything. There were no more shots and when he looked out again Wilton had gone. 'Dammit!' He stuck the gun into his belt, and went back to help Barbara and Fisher.

Barbara had climbed out of their prison by herself and was squatting by Fisher, tying a piece of her petti-coat round his arm.

'Marshal, what's going on?' the deputy asked.

'Are you badly wounded?'

'No, sir. What's. . . ?'

'Never mind! I'm going after him. Barbara, you stay here with Pat and tell him everything. I'll get someone to come up to stay with you.'

Barbara nodded. 'Nora, please.'

'Yes, sir, but . . .' Fisher began but Doyle had gone.

He raced out of the church and down through the cemetery. Then he came to a halt. There was no sign of the man. He'd gone again. He couldn't lose him this time. He couldn't! He wouldn't!

CHAPTER TWENTY-ONE

Judd had been surprised but pleased when he found Ben Hattersley waiting for him outside the boarding-house. They had made good progress, only stopping when the horses needed to, riding long into the night and starting again before dawn. All the same Judd was fretful and now he was relieved to see that Ashby appeared quiet in the late-morning sun.

'Jubal! Mr Judd!'

It was Doyle. On the other side of the street, looking hot and bothered. Hell and damnation! Something had happened. Doyle raced across the road towards the two men, almost getting knocked down by a horse-drawn wagon and earning himself a mouthful of abuse from the driver who had to swerve to miss him.

'It was Stroud!' he yelled. 'Stroud was Wilton!'

Judd had guessed as much and didn't need to waste time asking unnecessary questions.

'Where is he?'

'He's gone. Only in the last few minutes. He can't be far.'

'He'll run again,' Hattersley said. 'Just like before.'

'We must get after him,' Doyle said. 'But I need a drink before we go. Me and Barbara have been his prisoners for the past couple of days.'

Judd raised his eyebrows but said nothing.

'And me and Ben need fresh horses. Let's get on down to the livery. Is Miss Geddings all right?'

'Yeah, she is now.'

They had almost reached the livery stable when Doctor Hicks, with that nose for knowing when something was going on, strode into view.

Doyle hailed him.

'Hey, Doc, have you seen the reverend?'

'Yes, yes I have. He was riding out of town. Looked like the devil was chasing him. I called to him but he didn't take any notice.'

Judd thought Hicks had had a lucky escape. If Wilton hadn't been in such a hurry he could easily have shot the doctor.

'What's going on?'

'No time to explain now,' Doyle said. 'But you might go on down to the church. Fisher and Barbara – er – Miss Geddings, need your help. And send someone to the hotel to tell Nora that Barbara – er – Miss Geddings, is safe.'

'All right.' Hicks hurried away. Perhaps he would learn something from Barbara.

With Judd at their head, the three men rode, fast, out of town. Judd quickly recognized the direction Wilton had taken as the way through the hills he'd ridden on the first part of his journey to Juniper Creek.

'Where's he likely to go?' Doyle asked.

'Where he went before,' Judd said. 'He's heading for the desert.'

Hattersley nodded.

'For some reason he feels at home there. And if we don't keep up we'll lose him like I did before.'

'There's no danger of that at the moment,' Judd pointed out. 'There's only the one road. Even if he goes into the trees he'll still have to come out at the bottom of the hill. And he can't be that far ahead of us.'

Hattersley said nothing. Once before he'd been sure of what Rufus Wilton would do. He'd been proved wrong. He hoped Judd wasn't going to be wrong now.

They were making good progress when disaster struck! Judd's horse stepped into a hole. It stumbled, almost throwing him.

'Dammit!' He dismounted to examine the horse's leg. While not lame it was obvious the animal couldn't be ridden hard or for long.

'What shall we do?' Doyle said, taking the opportunity to have a drink of water from his canteen. He wiped the sweat from his face at the same time.

Judd glanced along their back trail. They'd travelled several miles from Ashby. In the time it would take to ride back to town, saddle up a fresh horse and get back here, Wilton would be too far ahead to catch him.

'We'll carry on,' he decided.

'You sure?'

'Yeah, Simon, it's the only way. We'll have to take it easy for a while but once we get out in the open we should see Wilton's dust. Be able to follow him that way.'

But they couldn't. Because when they reached the bottom of the hill, they lost Wilton's trail. There was no sign of him.

Up till then Judd, together with Hattersley, who had lost none of his skills, had managed to follow the tracks of the killer's horse, as he kept it to a gallop down the road. Wilton hadn't stopped to try and hide his tracks but had just concentrated on putting distance between himself and his pursuers.

Just as they emerged from the trees the road branched into two. One way led across the valley, the other merged into rocks and another stand of trees.

There the tracks vanished.

'Oh hell!' Hattersley exclaimed in disgust. 'I don't believe it.'

None of them did. How could Wilton have disappeared?

'The bastard's done it again!'

Judd knew that the road across the meadow led to the open country and eventually to the desert. It was the way he'd taken.

It was the obvious way for Wilton to take as well.

But had Wilton done so?

'Where does the other way go?' he asked.

'Round the bottom of the hill and back to Ashby.' Doyle paused as Judd glanced up sharply. 'You don't think he's gone back there, do you? Why would he?

Surely all he's concerned about is escaping?'

Judd gave his head a little shake.

'I don't know. He doesn't behave like anyone else.'

'He did mention wanting to get his own back on several people in Ashby,' Doyle said in a fretful tone. Then he broke off, his face turning white.

'I don't know,' Judd said again. 'I can't see Wilton taking a chance on doing something like that when he knows his true identity has been discovered. On the other hand it's clear he likes taking chances.'

'Oh hell!'

While they were talking, Hattersley had urged his horse a little way up the track leading to Ashby. Suddenly he stopped and swung himself out of the saddle, bending over the ground. He beckoned the other two to him.

'Look.' He sounded excited. He pointed to the print of a horse's hoof in the soft earth beneath an overhanging rock. 'This is Wilton's. He thinks he's clever but this time he ain't been quite damn clever enough!'

'He is doubling back to Ashby!' Doyle exclaimed with something like panic in his voice. 'Christ! Barbara! If he sees her he might shoot her.' An awful thought struck him. 'He might even be going back to make her his prisoner again. We've got to get there. And quick!'

Judd said: 'You two go on.'

'Hell, Jubal, we can't leave you out here,' Doyle objected.

' 'Course you can. You need to get back fast and my horse is too hurt for that. I'll be all right.'

'What will you do?'

'I'll follow on behind you. Don't worry. And, Simon, when you reach Ashby don't take any risks. Get help if you need it.'

'We will.' But it was obvious Doyle was too concerned over Barbara to listen. 'C'mon, Ben, let's go.'

Judd watched as they rode away. They were soon lost to his view. Was Wilton really going back to Ashby? It seemed a stupid thing to do and while Wilton might be mad, he wasn't stupid. Yet that was where his tracks led. Or was he fooling them again? He stared at the trees on the far side of the valley. There was nothing to be seen. Was Wilton there, watching him, laughing, because he was yet again going to escape?

Judd decided to make sure. He gigged his horse into a slow walk.

Doyle set a fast pace all the way back into Ashby. He was sweating, heart pounding, as he hoped and prayed Wilton wasn't too far ahead of him and Hattersley – he couldn't be! he couldn't be! – wreaking havoc in his town.

Once they got there, he expected to see all sorts of dreadful things – dead bodies, crowds gathered in Main Street, blood!

Instead all was quiet.

Puzzled, still afraid, Doyle rode first to his office. It was empty. And then to Doctor Hicks's place.

Hicks was there with Barbara and Nora and Pat Fisher. The deputy was bandaged up, quite liking being fussed over.

'What's the matter?' Barbara looked up in alarm as the two men burst into the room.

'Have you caught him?' Hicks asked.

'No. We thought he was coming back here.'

'Oh!' Barbara said and caught hold of Nora's hand, clutching it tightly.

'Don't worry, Barbara – er – Miss Geddings,' Doyle said. 'I won't let anything happen to you.'

But it didn't seem as if Doyle would get the chance to protect Barbara because Hicks said:

'We haven't seen him. Everything is quiet.'

'Oh, Christ.' Doyle looked at Hattersley, his heart sinking. 'He tricked us.' As Wilton had tricked people all his life. 'He wasn't coming back here after all. We did exactly what he wanted us to.'

'And,' Hattersley added, 'Marshal Judd is out there alone and we've got no way to warn him.'

CHAPTER
TWENTY-TWO

It was quiet and cool when Judd entered the shade of the trees. Here, he saw, were stands of rocks amongst the undergrowth. He didn't go very far before stopping. His horse was becoming lamer with each step it took and Judd began to wonder whether it would make it all the way back to Ashby. There was little point in going any further because it didn't seem Wilton was anywhere around.

Just to be sure, he dismounted and hunkered down to study the ground.

No, nothing.

'*YEEOOUUWW!*'

It wasn't a yell, nor a screech, but a howl! A human yowl!

Startling, shocking!

With the surprise of the eerie sound, Judd's heart missed several beats. All the same he moved quickly. But not quite quickly enough. Even as he was clawing for his gun and rising at the same time, a shadow leapt towards him from its hiding-place in the rocks. And before he could get to his feet, Rufus Wilton jumped on to his back and sent him sprawling to the ground.

Despite the breath being knocked out of his body, Judd rolled over, trying to get up. Only to be kicked hard in the chest and sent sprawling again. Judd glanced up. Wilton kicked him twice more and laughed. Then he drew his gun, pointing it at Judd, daring him to move.

'Seen y'all chasing me,' Wilton sneered. 'Set a trap for you. Damn funny when you fell for it.' He sounded proud, as if he wasn't surprised. 'Was that old Hattersley with you?'

Judd didn't waste his breath in reply.

'Always was stupid. Glad you ain't so easy to outwit. It makes a change to have someone as clever as me chasing me. Don't often happen. If it weren't for you I could've gotten away. But I'm glad you come after me. Now I can kill you. You're gonna die. Might even bury your body so everyone wonders where you are. Pity I ain't a real preacher but say your prayers anyway, Mr United States Marshal.'

His finger tightened on the trigger.

Judd's hand had scrabbled on the ground and closed on a stone. Now he threw it at Wilton. It spoiled his aim. The bullet went wide. And at the same time Judd heaved himself up and flung himself at the man.

They went down in a blur of bodies, arms and legs flailing. The gun flew from Wilton's hand. On the ground they exchanged blows and kicks. Wilton was a strong and quick fighter, willing to use dirty tricks. But so was Judd.

And Judd was no longer afraid of the man. Cursed himself for ever having been. Wilton wasn't an invincible demon but flesh and blood, the same as him; no better a fighter. He could be beaten.

Wilton, not content with using his strength and speed, lowered his guard to twist his head round and try to bite Judd's hand. He didn't just want to win the fight, he wanted to inflict pain. Instead it gave Judd the opening he needed. He balled his other hand into a fist and slammed it as hard as possible into Wilton's jaw. Bone shattered. Several teeth broke. The man's eyes glazed over and he went slack on top of Judd.

Breathing heavily Judd pushed Wilton off him and stood up. Wilton rolled on to his stomach and lay still. Judd waited for a moment but the man didn't move.

Quickly Judd looked round. Wilton's gun was on the other side of the path, well out of harm's way. He reached behind him for the handcuffs he kept attached to his belt, glancing at the killer.

'Come on.' He poked Wilton with his toe.

Nothing.

Judd bent down to haul Wilton up. As he turned him on to his back the man's eyes shot open and with another howl he brought one hand up. Fast. Judd caught a glimpse of the shiny steel of a Bowie knife.

His one thought was to get out of the way. He reared back. Somehow twisted his body round far enough, so that instead of Wilton embedding the blade in his chest, it struck the fleshy part of his upper arm.

Crying out with the shock of the sudden pain, Judd fell backwards. Wilton leapt up and, screeching, came after him, hefting the knife aloft.

Just in time Judd swivelled out of the way. Carried forward by his own momentum, Wilton stumbled. Judd realized Wilton's gun lay close by. He reached for it. Picked it up. And as Wilton righted himself and came dashing for him again Judd, still on his back, raised the gun. And pulled the trigger. Twice.

Both bullets caught Wilton high in the chest, stopped him in his all-out rush.

With a scream of surprise and hurt, Wilton jerked backwards. He dropped the knife as he grabbed for the wounds, from which blood was pouring. Falling at the same time, he landed heavily. Sighed once. And didn't move again.

By the time Judd picked himself up and went over to him, Wilton was dead.

It was over. Judd sighed. Thank God.

'You're lucky,' Doctor Hicks said, after he'd patched up Judd's wound. 'You'll soon recover the full use of your arm.'

Judd was relieved. Anything else and he might not have been able to continue as a lawman.

'You know,' Hicks went on, 'I can't believe it that our preacher, the good Reverend Stroud, was a killer. But,' he added with a sigh, 'I never did like that man! He was always too good to be true.'

Judd and Doyle looked at one another and

grinned. Doctor Hicks was in his element. He would once again be the one everyone went to for help and advice.

The two lawmen accompanied one another out into the street.

'Ben Hattersley's staying the night and going home tomorrow,' Doyle said as they strolled towards the hotel. 'He said now he knows Wilton is truly dead he can put the past behind him.'

'What about Barbara? Do you know what she's decided to do?'

'She's staying in Ashby, for the time being anyway. I must say that after everything that happened I was surprised.'

'Barbara is a brave young lady.'

Doyle nodded. 'I was also pleased.' He lowered his eyes so Judd wouldn't see the happiness in them but there was no hiding his reddened face.

Judd grinned. Doyle obviously hoped that Barbara would, one day, return the feelings the marshal had for her. Perhaps she would. Perhaps she already did.

'And you, Jubal, what will you do?'

'I'll leave as soon as everything here is settled.'

Did Doyle look relieved? Pleased that he would get his town back?

For his part Judd knew he would be pleased to leave Ashby and its uncomfortable memories behind. Wilton was dead and Judd wanted to forget all about him and his villainy. He hoped he would never have to go up against anyone like him again.